A Special Kind of Heartache

A cozy mystery rooted in the South Carolina Lowcountry

Laura Elizabeth

For more information and to get to know the author, visit:

TheIslandMysteries.com

Cover design by Rick Nease
RickNeaseArt.com

Published by Front Edge Mystery, an imprint of Front Edge Publishing.

Do you have a mystery you'd love to share with the world? For more information about publishing with Front Edge, please visit FrontEdgePublishing.com or contact info@ FrontEdgePublishing.com.

Front Edge Publishing, LLC
No. 234, 42807 Ford Road
Canton, MI
48162

Front Edge Publishing books are available for discount bulk purchases for events, corporate use and small groups. Special editions, including books with corporate logos, personalized covers and customized interiors are available for purchase. For more information, contact Front Edge Publishing at info@FrontEdgePublishing.com.

To Jay, Meghan, and Colin

Thank you for being the people who share my excitement of arriving at our special place and my sadness to leave it. For all the oyster shells, pinecones, dirt roads, quiet moments, happy times, amazing memories and dreams to come ... for all the island magic, thank you.

Chapter 1

The beach was starting to empty, and I knew what time it was. The sun still warmed me, but there was just that hint of a cooler breeze on my face. The tide was coming in, pushing those of us who liked to set up our chairs where our feet can touch the water while we read closer to the dunes. The ocean was depositing more shells as it inched up the beach. The sun was still shining, and the wind was blowing, but it was time to shake out the beach blankets and head home. Spending the day on Rosemont Beach, Mongin Island, could anything be better?

This beach, and all of Mongin Island, never suffers the same fate as its neighbors. It is unspoiled, restorative, and allows you to experience it in your own way. Large crowds, busy roads, traffic, and noise don't exist here. We are all grateful for that. As Mongin Island is bridgeless, a visit here is intentional. You choose to come here, and you come knowing life is different. There are few cars, no grocery stores, no movie theaters, and none of the things you find in other tourist spots. You come here anyway and choose the beauty of your surroundings. You let the peacefulness of this island work its magic. The old, tall oaks with their protective canopies and Spanish moss, the beautiful pink and red sunsets, the dirt roads, the hidden spots of nature's bounty, the untouched, almost forgotten hideaways are Mongin Island's treasures. You come for these things, and you leave better for having experienced them.

There is something about living on an island. Time moves at its own pace, but there is still a rhythm to the seasons. Today there were no kites flying overhead. There were no sandcastles constructed near the water's edge. I could not hear the bits and pieces of made-up games. On this sunny Friday, the beach was noticeably absent of any school-aged children and the beachgoers who were dotted along this several-mile stretch were far too distant from each other to do any-thing except wave. It was definitely September.

This day was perfect. It was exactly what I needed to start decom-pressing from the busier summer months. I survived my first summer as both a full-time Mongin Island resident and a new small business owner. Books & Brew, the island bookstore I opened earlier this year, has quickly become a community meeting place and a spot frequently visited by tourists. Its location is ideal, as it is close to the ferry docks. It is convenient for people to pop in and grab something for a boat ride, day at the beach, or just to fill the time until their accommoda-tions are ready. The store has a large front porch where people gather, sit a spell, and visit with others. Introductions are made and friend-ships are strengthened here. Inside there are nooks where customers settle in to sip freshly brewed tea and get lost in their selections. We have a few overstuffed club chairs in the middle of the main room, where some folks read, and others come to people-watch. It's called the Trading Floor, a room I dedicated to book-swapping, where many book clubs and other groups gather. The long, wood farm table and mismatched chairs create an inviting space, and the informality of this room is the perfect environment for all kinds of discussions. People have begun to make it their own. Sharing my vision with this community and watching them build on it has been truly a labor of love.

The summer had been busy by Mongin Island standards. Tripp, the store's only other employee and my right hand, was indispensable. We worked many more hours than either of us had intended, but we both enjoyed building this business. He is a retired schoolteacher who loves books and loves people. Tripp listens to customers, often finding books that fit them perfectly. When we receive donations for the Trading Floor, Tripp examines each one. If something catches his eye for a customer, he suggests it to them on their next visit. He connects with people and gets such joy from building these relationships. We found each other when we both needed something on which to focus. Our mutual love of reading brought us together as work colleagues, but his warm, caring nature and strong character made us friends. Tripp runs our store's website, and together we brainstorm many ideas for reading groups and other events that help make Books & Brew part of this community. It had been a tiring but rewarding summer.

I didn't come to Mongin Island to open a bookstore. Many years earlier, my husband and I impulsively bought a beach home on the Rosemont Resort property after visiting and becoming enchanted. We planned to retire on the island someday. However, I was lost in my former life after Rob's sudden death. I retreated to Mongin Island, feeling as if I was coming home.

I used to say I came to put the pieces of me back together again. Now, after living through the first year without my husband, I realize that was not really true. That statement implied I would somehow return to my former self, and something would build me back to what I used to be. I know now I will never be that person again. In reality, I came to Mongin Island to learn to live a life without the man who had shared nearly four decades with me. Mongin Island had helped heal me, and I found a new purpose. Little by little, this community encouraged me to take small steps forward. This was now my home, and I was grateful.

While Tripp managed the store, it was my turn to have a day off. We would both be at the store the next day and intended to spend the morning planning for the upcoming holidays, knowing that they would be our best chance for a robust sales season. Ordering books and scheduling events were top agenda items. To prepare, I analyzed our quarterly sales trends and inventory. We had a lot to discuss. At that moment, it was a wonderful treat to sit by the water's edge, read the latest from one of my favorite authors, bask in the warm sun, and enjoy a Mongin Island day.

Walking back to my abandoned beach blanket, I could barely hear my phone ringing from the bottom of my canvas tote bag. I set my ringtone to "old car horn", not because I loved it so much but because it was one I could usually hear over the ocean waves or as I drove down the bumpy, unpaved island roads in my golf cart. Before I could dig my phone out, the ringing stopped. The voicemail chime rang as I finished folding the blanket and gathering my sandals. I listened to the message as I walked to my cart and smiled when I heard Barb's voice.

"Hey, where are you? Wait, I bet I know where you are—at the beach, reading. It is much too nice of a day for you to be inside. I was calling to find out if you wanted to grab dinner tonight. Give me a buzz when you get this. Okay? Thanks, and bye. Please don't wait too long, I am already starving. Okay, bye for real now."

When I used to visit the island, Barb had been an acquaintance. Since moving here full-time, she has become a very close friend. Barb's ability to embrace "the now", and to live presently—without worrying about tomorrow or yesterday—pushes me forward at times when I'm stuck in how things were or how I thought they should be. Barb's ability to wing it has brought so much unexpected joy to my daily life and taught me to celebrate that, to live more on island time. To Barb, I wasn't Nicholas' or Meredith's mom, Rob's wife, a former consultant, a PTA volunteer, a work colleague, or a professional reference. I was just me, and she welcomed that. For her part, I only knew Barb as a Mongin Island community member. I wasn't tied to what she used to be. During this season of my life, this friendship had been particularly meaningful to me.

She answered my return call on the first ring. "Are you free tonight?"

I sensed an opportunity brewing, "I am. I planned to finish the last tomatoes I bought from the Community Farm. How does a panzanella salad sound to you?"

"Yum, that sounds amazing! I haven't made it over to the mainland for groceries, so it's pretty sparse at my house. I was thinking about grabbing something at the Beach Club. If you're sure you want to cook, I will bring dessert. I've got just the thing for us. Sounds like this could be an elastic waist pants kind of night," Barb answered, and I could tell she was smiling too.

"Yoga pants it is!" I said. "The salad will be quick, so yes, let's eat at my house. Give me thirty minutes to rinse off and get things started. See you soon!"

It didn't take long to set the table on the screened porch and toss the tomatoes in olive oil, fresh garlic, herbs, lemon juice, and Dijon mustard. The bread was toasting, and I had a bottle of wine chilling. Buddy, my recently adopted black Labrador retriever mix, watched all the activity from one of his favorite woven kitchen rugs. When I saw him lift his head and look toward the back door, I knew Barb had arrived. He is such a cozy companion. Buddy rarely barks, loves making new friends, and is blissfully unaware of personal space. He often places himself next to customers or visitors and waits patiently to be introduced. At the same time, he often successfully senses if someone isn't a dog fan and keeps his distance. Fortunately, we don't often encounter those people, as Mongin Island is very dog friendly.

I watched him trot happily to the door, sit down with his tail sweeping the floor, and wait for Barb. "There's our boy, hi Buddy!" she greeted him as she knocked and came in. "Hi Carr, smells delicious in here!" True to her nature, she was a bundle of energy. She slipped off her shoes, rubbed Buddy's head, and unpacked her supplies all at the same time.

"Look what I have here! You're going to love and hate me. Are you ready for this? Stracciatella gelato from Nonna Marie's and, of course, our favorite, java chip. I was over on the mainland the other day and had to pick up my treat supplies. Goes well with our dinner, it was meant to be!" She quickly loaded the goods into my freezer. Of course, she also had something for Buddy, and he was happily munching the cookie she slipped him.

We were soon settled at the round table, catching up on the last few days and enjoying our meal together. We never run out of things to talk about; there are never any awkward silences. As we cleared the plates, we started to think about weekend plans. "I have five check-ins tomorrow, believe it or not. All my current properties have arrivals, except the one down by the county dock. The rest will have arrivals throughout the day tomorrow," Barb reported.

After moving to Mongin Island decades ago, Barb started a property management company and now had many island rental properties in her portfolio. People often rely on her to guide them in selecting just the right vacation spot, and she frequently helps them plan their visits by providing island insights and recommendations. "It will be busy, that's for sure. Fortunately, three groups will be here for at least two weeks. The house next to the Inn is rented for six weeks, so at least next Saturday won't be filled with check-outs."

"Are these all-new visitors or will we have some familiar faces?" I asked. "Great to have so many visitors, even as summer fades away!"

"We will have a busy September and October on the island, for sure. Most of our properties are booked back-to-back. That will be good for Books & Brew, too. I bet you will have a lot of traffic."

"You're right about that. I am a little concerned about the winter months. We had so much momentum this spring and summer. It's been so busy that I actually was able to get a little lost in it all. I have to admit, I am concerned about having a quiet shop. I don't think that will be good for me."

Barb watched me as I spoke. I couldn't tell what she was thinking. She briefly placed her hand over mine and then gently said, "It may be exactly what is good for you, but you likely don't want to take that medicine." Expertly, before I could protest, she shifted back to answering my earlier question, "We have only two repeat visitors, and the other three are all new groups. I got lucky with this batch. They are all coming on different ferries so I can spend some time with each group."

"I saw what you did there, don't think I missed it," I replied as I got down our favorite cobalt blue bowls from the glass-front corner cabinet. It was time for something sweet.

"Believe me, by now, I know full well there is nothing you miss," Barb said as I scooped out our gelato.

Chapter 2

Tripp and I had already been busy working away the early morning. We were several mugs of tea into our holiday ordering when we heard the crunch of tires pulling into the store's oyster shell tabby parking lot.

"Tripp, it's nearly time to open! How did it get so late so quickly?" I stood up and gathered our laptops, mugs, and breakfast plates. There were still a few things to do to be ready for customers. People tended to stop into Books & Brew before starting their day. As we learned sales patterns, we found that our days were structured around ferry schedules and other island events. On Saturdays, the store was often busy as soon as we opened, so we needed to be ready to hit the ground running. Today was proving to be like so many other Saturdays.

"Looks like it's Helen who just pulled in," Tripp said as he unlocked the glass and wood door, his tall frame blocking me from seeing around him.

He went to straighten the rockers on the porch. The sudden burst of energy woke Buddy from his first of many morning naps. He hopped down from his favorite comfy chair and trotted happily out the door to greet our visitor, his black ears flapping with each step. In just a few months of being a bookstore dog, he had claimed his seat, and our regular customers knew that even if it was momentarily unoccupied, they still better choose another place to sit. The chair closest to the cash register was Buddy's. The only person he would willingly share "his" chair with was Jacob, a boy who recently moved to the island and who often swung by Books & Brew for something new to read. Like this particular chair, Buddy had claimed Jacob, too.

"Helen, good to see you!" I called as I finished brewing a carafe of tea and freshening up the store.

As Helen settled into one of the overstuffed club chairs in the center of the room, Tripp grabbed the broom from our utility closet and went to sweep the pine needles scattered around the porch.

"I was telling Tripp that the 9:00 a.m. ferry was at capacity. I took the first boat to the mainland today to grab a few groceries and almost didn't get a seat on the return trip. I think we will be busy this week. I thought the season was just about over, but it seems we are still going strong." A tinge of annoyance was right under the surface of her casual words.

"Barb was saying the same thing last night."

"Well, personally, I am exhausted by all the hustle and bustle, I just ..."

Helen was interrupted by the tinkling bell that hung above the store's door, announcing the arrival of the first batch of customers. They immediately filled the store with canvas tote bags and loud voices.

"Good morning! Welcome to Books & Brew," I greeted the three women warmly. "Welcome to Mongin Island! Is this your first visit?"

"I've been here before, years ago. I'm Mary Frances—nice to meet you." The tallest woman stepped forward and moved her long, curly brown hair over one shoulder. We shook hands as she attempted to smile, but she didn't look happy. Her companions stood with their arms crossed and offered nothing. Books & Brew was suddenly pulsating with an uncomfortable vibe.

"I am Carr, and this is my store. Please let me know if I can help you find something or if you would like any book suggestions." Before I finished my introduction, the group had split up, heading to different corners. They were all dressed in various athletic wear and sneakers, looking like they could sprint out the door in a blink of an eye.

Helen and I exchanged a questioning look as she stood to leave. "Exhausted, I am telling you." Her copper-colored hair swung from side to side as she shook her head, then she waved over her shoulder as she walked out.

Helen was a long-time island resident. She purchased her first home here before any of the resort development boomed, when the island only had a couple of dozen permanent residents. As the seasons passed, her patience for the flexibility needed to live side by side with the influx of tourists was in shorter supply. She was no longer energized by our visitors' new faces and stories. She was less interested in the possibilities they brought to our island. As a business owner and a former tourist, I did not share her opinion. However, I learned months ago it was often a good idea to keep your thoughts to yourself when you disagreed with Helen. She rolled out her version of a welcome mat on her terms when she wanted to. Today was not one of those days.

Although other new arrivals from the early boat and several of my regulars had stopped by, the store was not so crowded that I missed my first customers' quiet departure. As I watched them climb into their rental cart, I saw an additional visitor join them. All four looked on in different directions, and the two assigned to the rear-facing seat each sat with their legs and arms crossed. I wondered what made them all so miserable at the start of their vacation on this sunny Saturday. In just a blink, they turned onto Old Port Passage Way. I needed to put them out of my mind. There was plenty to do, and whatever was bothering them was something they had to fix, not me.

Sometime after lunch, Tripp said what I had been thinking, "For such a beautiful beach day, we were surprisingly busy!"

"You're not kidding. Did you see that Mrs. Greenwich stopped by? I know you were helping some folks over by the nonfiction shelves when we were chatting, but did you catch any of our conversation?"

"I saw her and thought I heard something about a book fair at the elementary school. Was that it?"

"I am so excited! Yes, that's it. As the school's principal, she's been tasked with choosing the main fundraiser this year. She asked if we would collaborate with her to do a book fair. Isn't that amazing? She thought we could target the early spring before the end-of-the-year craziness starts. That will give us plenty of time to plan, buy books, and all that stuff. I told her we would do some research and email her to set up a time for us to meet. What do you think?"

Tripp was just as excited as I was. It would be Mongin's first-ever book fair, and another opportunity to make choosing books a fun activity for the island's children. We had plenty of ideas. We were deeply debating his suggestion to add a bake sale to the event when Barb arrived.

"Hey, Barb, are all your arrivals already settled? You're done early!" I greeted her as she got comfortable next to Buddy. Her shoes were already off, and she curled her legs into the seat of the club chair. I noticed she was wearing her "good" T-shirt, the one gifted to her by a visitor last year. It brought out the blue in her eyes. She ran her tanned fingers through her short blonde hair, pulling it away from her face as she sometimes does.

"Tell the boss here that all the kids would love a bake sale at the school book fair," Tripp blurted out before she could answer.

"Book fair? Here at the store or the school? This is news. My vote is for cake, but I want to hear more." She took a long drink from her water bottle and continued, "I am wiped out. Things went pretty well, almost everyone settled pretty quickly. It was great to see some repeat visitors. They are thrilled to be back and already making plans for next year."

"Sounds like Mongin Island already has worked its magic," I said.

"Not for everyone, that's for sure. There's a girls' trip I am not sure about. I have to tell you; they are the most miserable group I've seen in years. It's a good thing they are in the four-bedroom beach cottage on the resort property. They each have their own space. Doesn't look promising if they are already on each other's nerves."

Tripp laughed, "Oh, we got a taste, first thing this morning, if we're talking about the same group. I think they stopped in right from the dock because their cart was loaded with their suitcases and all their supplies. I saw one of the ladies just standing in the parking lot, glued to her phone. The rest of them buzzed around her. Then, they piled into their cart looking like they had each just swallowed a lemon."

Tripp painted such a vivid picture that we all burst out laughing.

"That is the perfect description, Tripp." Barb wiped her eyes and continued, "I've been doing this for years. You both have heard my stories of some memorable guests. There have been a few groups who probably shouldn't ever travel together again, that's for sure. But this crew? They remind me of those horrible school days when I didn't get picked for the team in gym class. You know what I mean? It's definitely three against one. It made me feel sorry for the blonde lady, although I have no idea what all of that nonsense is about."

"Enough about the sourpusses!" she continued. "We do have some visitors I think you both *will* enjoy." She filled us in on the other groups she had welcomed earlier. "Tripp, do you remember the Haverils from North Carolina? Carr, I'm not sure you've met them yet. They usually visit in the early fall. You may have missed them last year. Well, anyway, they rented the house next to the Inn for six weeks. Dan Haveril has been painting a series of watercolors focused on shore birds. He will be working on them during their stay. Looks like that sunroom at the back of the house will be his temporary studio."

Tripp and I looked at each other. I knew we were thinking the same thing, but Tripp asked first. "How about we invite him for an artist talk here at the store, and we can highlight our books on regional birds?"

"You two have an event for every occasion! Give them a day or so to settle in, and then you may bump into them on the resort property. Who knows? They may wander in here before then."

"I always like to highlight our local authors and of course, any Mongin Island books. Tripp, if we get this lined up in the next week or two, we may want to sort through the Trading Floor to see if we have any relevant books people can swap. This way, everyone can participate if they want. We can pull those and hold them until the event to make sure there is a good selection for everyone."

"I'm thinking of several books that could work," he said as he left us to start exploring the shelves he had in mind. Knowing Tripp, he would search until he found at least a few things we could offer for this potential event. Something new would now be on his radar as he sorted any future donations we received.

He and I feel strongly that store events are for everyone. We offer community events. It doesn't matter if you purchase a book or if you just come to socialize. The most important thing to me is that everyone feels welcome here. As a result, our events have quite a following, and usually, the store is at capacity. Sometimes guests spill out to the front porch, and we have to prop open the door so presentations can be heard there, too. I love it. It's like having more guests than space at your Thanksgiving dinner table, and you have to get creative to offer everyone a seat. To me, there was no such thing as too many people who want to enjoy an evening together at Books & Brew.

"So anyway, Dan is great, and I think we are going to have a busy week. Forgot to ask you, are you doing the chili cook-off at the fire station tomorrow?"

"Is that tomorrow? No, I can't make chili to save my life! That was one of Rob's specialties, actually." Talking about him always felt good to me, and Barb was someone with whom I could share a story about my husband without it being uncomfortable. Some people hesitated to mention him either because they feared my reaction or wanted to avoid their discomfort. Barb was different. She knew I was strong enough, I was okay enough, and that I wanted to keep his memory alive by occasionally weaving him into our conversations.

"Since you're not participating, how about you share one or two of his secret ingredients with me? I enter this contest every year, and the closest I came to winning was as second runner-up. That must have been at least three years ago!"

"Second runner-up? That's a very nice way of saying third place, definitely sounds better." I laughed with her. "I'm afraid I won't be much help to you with his recipe, but you may want to text Meredith.

She used to help her dad, and they both enjoyed experimenting together. You have her number, right?"

"I do, and I am not kidding, I want to win this year. I will text your sweet daughter and see if I can get some tips from her. I need to head to the mainland and get some groceries for this shindig, so I better get going if I am going to catch the next boat. I will head over to the station mid-afternoon to set up—after my prize-winning concoction has a chance to simmer for a few hours, of course."

"Well, yes, of course. We will be there, once the shop closes, to see the judges pin the first place blue ribbon on your trusty slow cooker."

We laughed together as Barb firmly crossed her fingers on both hands and waved them above her head. She then stood up to leave. "I will see you there. Let's hope my luck is about to change."

Tripp beat me to Books & Brew on Sunday morning and already had a carafe of English breakfast tea brewed. By this point in the season, we knew the drill, and we each got started on our usual tasks to prepare us for the day. The store would open soon. We worked in a companionable silence, interrupted now and then by Buddy's gentle snoring. He had found a cozy sunbeam that warmed him on the area rug in the center of the room.

Right before opening, I poured two steaming mugs of tea and joined Tripp on the front porch.

"Let's sit for these last few quiet minutes before the day begins." I invited him to grab a seat in one of the wooden teak rockers that lined our front porch. Their warm wood color was already starting to gray. The humid salt air had weathered these recent additions, and they now looked like they had always been casually a part of this porch's decor.

We were deciding what we wanted to add to the few planters on the porch steps. These pots were made by Boyd, the island potter, years ago, and were favorites of mine. Their stone and blue pattern announced what customers would experience as they walked into Books & Brew. Indigo blue combined with an otherwise natural color palette was my way of inviting the beautiful Mongin outdoors into this shop, creating an almost seamless environment.

"Don't you have some ideas you clipped from your magazines? I thought there was a folder on your desk labeled 'flowerpot fillers'?" Tripp reminded me.

"You're right, goodness, I'm going to grab that, and we can settle this. I can tell you right now, I want to get some of those ornamental pepper plants. I think they are so fun!"

Before I got too far, we both heard the crunch of tires and knew our first customers were arriving. Barb's beach cottage girls' trip visitors were back at Books & Brew. Tripp greeted them from the porch, and I knew we both hoped this wouldn't be the second day in a row to start with cranky customers.

"Welcome back," I said as they filled the main room.

The vibe was different today as they stood together in a half-circle. "Hello, again." Mary Frances smiled broadly. "We came to stock up on some beach reads. Glad you are open so early on this beautiful day."

"This is Tracy, Annabelle, and Carrie," she pointed to her friends as she introduced them. Mary Frances was the tallest of the group and we knew without her saying a word that she was their leader. Her long brown hair swung past her shoulders. She wore even casual clothes in an orderly fashion. Everything was in its right place—her hair, her sunglasses on her head, her layered beach coverup, the nail polish that matched her clothes.

Tracy was the opposite. She looked like she had a pack of dynamite crammed into her short frame. She wore no makeup, jewelry, or accessories of any kind. From what she was wearing, you couldn't tell if she was going to the beach or ready to mow the lawn. Her short blonde hair was styled in a "wash and go" cut, there was nothing fussy about her, but she radiated the energy of someone absorbing her surroundings, processing her observations in real time.

Annabelle moved almost regally and reminded me of a long-ago famous actress. She was lovely, balancing speaking confidently but not needing to be the center of attention. She knew what she wanted to say and would wait to say it until the time was right. Like Mary Frances, she also had long brown hair, but hers had a ray of highlights that shimmered as she turned to take in the room.

It was Carrie who was the most mysterious. Not quite as tall as Mary Frances, she still stood a few inches taller than me and as I looked up to greet her, I could tell something was weighing on her. She smiled and spoke kindly but there was a heaviness to her, like a weight was on each of her tanned shoulders, which peeked out from her turquoise blue tank top. She was dressed for the beach and I silently wished she would find tranquility in being near the water for the day.

We exchanged a few pleasantries before I pointed them to the genres they were interested in reading. In short order, they selected and purchased their books. They were on their way as other customers began to arrive.

"These will get us started. Thanks, I know we will see you soon!" Annabelle called over her shoulder as they left the store. They moved almost as one, and I sensed they likely had been friends for years. There was that long-time familiarity with each other, the connectedness that needed no explanation, no pause, no anticipation.

Customers came and went, and with them, the day passed. A few of my younger customers needed books for school reports, and parents were stocking up on things that would help them pass the time at soccer games, play rehearsals, and the activities that came to life at the beginning of a school year. It was definitely September.

Before long, we were piled in our carts and joined many other community members at the fire station.

Chief Lancaster greeted us by the door and handed us a scorecard, "Here you go. Now, be honest. We need fair judging at this cook-off. The winner gets the coveted chili trophy." He was speaking to no one in particular, and no one answered him directly.

We all knew the winner, like the other contestants, would receive invitations to prepare chili for many island events during the next few months. Regardless of the votes, participants would be called into action for school fundraisers, beach cleanups, golf tournaments, and other community-shared experiences, which made this pageantry even more enjoyable. Everyone would win tonight, even the second runner-up.

"Hello again!" I saw Mary Frances, Tracy, Annabelle, and Carrie in line, waiting to taste test and sample the offerings.

"This is such a small-town fun event," Annabelle said warmly while the rest of her group moved to the next sample station. Her beautiful hazel eyes shined with happiness, inviting me to share the moment with her.

"It is! This is an annual event, and people look forward to it. It is pretty competitive from a bragging rights perspective. It seems—"

"Is there a prize?" Carrie interrupted as she scanned the room and shifted her long legs in place. I couldn't tell if her impatience was directed at me, the noise, her surroundings, or her companions.

"There is the cauldron trophy, over on the shelf near the door. It's a traveling prize where the winner has to bring it back and pass it along next year." I usually enjoyed it when visitors wanted to become part of our local traditions.

"No money? Just that?"

"Just that and our admiration, I guess."

She turned and walked away while she looked down at her phone. I wondered how she could navigate the crowd with her eyes glued to the screen and her thumbs moving in all directions as she continued her text conversation. She seemed distracted, physically present but a million miles away in her thoughts.

Tracy crossed her arms across her and spoke quickly, "Please, excuse her, I'm sorry. We are at a loss. I don't know how to explain this. We've all known each other for years, and done a million things together, including a lot of girls' trips. But this time, well, I am not sure about this time. This has definitely not started the way I thought it would. I thought we were doing better today, but now, well, now I see that's not the case. She won't open up; she doesn't tell us what's going on. She is completely checked out. Looks like we are in for another night of it, girls."

"No need to apologize to me, please don't worry on my account. Mongin Island doesn't work for everyone."

"I don't think it's Mongin Island. I think it's Carrie, and I think the same thing would have happened no matter where we were. Her so-called love life is consuming her. She is more interested in that than being with us. You know … um, us, her friends for the past few decades. The ones she has known practically all her life." Her round face was growing redder as she spoke.

She continued, but louder now. I couldn't tell if this was because the community was quickly gathering or because we struck a nerve. "She is on those dating apps, swiping this way and swiping that way. She is more interested in chatting with these unknown guys, these strangers, than with us. I don't know how I will make it through the week. It is already on my last nerve. She has nothing to say to us. Well, nothing nice, that is."

Tracy was looking at Mary Frances as she spoke, but Annabelle spoke first.

"Well, Carrie has barely spoken more than a handful of words to me. She was the maid of honor at my wedding, after all. You would think she would ask how Todd is doing since his surgery. I mean, he *is* my husband, the least she could do is ask." Her gaze landed on her shoes. I wanted to see her face as she said these words. I couldn't tell from her voice if she was disappointed, angry, or just sad her long-time friend seemed to be slipping away.

"I think it hit her hard, after her last birthday, that she isn't in a long-term relationship. Tracy, since you've been married three times, you may not get this." Mary Frances teased her, trying to lighten the mood.

Tracy was having none of it. "I'm not buying it. We have seen her through some bad relationships with some pretty awful choices. Let's face it, we all have had our share of things that didn't work out, but come on, this is next level, even for her. She has waited this long to find Mr. Right, couldn't she just wait a few more days? We planned this trip months ago and all agreed the girls' trips were something we wanted to continue. She wasn't interested in any of the planning stuff we did, and she has gotten worse since we left the mainland. Carrie has really just been nasty to all of us. I am sick of it. Nothing is good enough, nothing is right. If I wanted to be criticized, second-guessed, and generally under the microscope, I could have just stayed home and gone to work."

They continued debating about when exactly Carrie stopped caring about their trip, and I silently but purposely lost track of them as I visited with other islanders. I needed to put some space between them and my own plan for the evening, which was simply to enjoy being with my friends and neighbors.

The chili judging was going to be tough this year. Every table in the firehouse was filled with a different concoction. The number of entries surpassed the past few years, and competition would be stiff. As we all considered our options, the room grew louder and was filled with the scents of different spices. Spirits were high. Children played impromptu games of tag and drew on the cement firehouse floor with pastel sidewalk chalk. The community band played some jazz numbers, and generally, it was happy chaos—until the prizes were awarded.

"First runner-up! I was robbed!" Barb blurted out when a canary yellow ribbon was stuck to her oval stainless slow cooker. She still received a hearty round of applause, but it was Helen who took home the top prize.

"Eat up! I have another batch warming in the station kitchen. There is plenty for everyone," she proudly announced. "Whatever doesn't go today, I can bring to the store tomorrow," she said more quietly to me. With that, our plans for tomorrow were made.

Chapter 3

"Hello? Are you open yet? Hello, Carr?"

The store lights were not on, but since the door was unlocked, the store was now open. My work would wait until later. I shut down my laptop and went to greet my visitor.

"Helen, hi! Let me get the lights for us."

"Am I too early?"

"No, you're right on time. Is this the chili delivery?"

"It is, and I can set up wherever you want. Thought I would start early so everything would be warmed by lunch. So, over here, is this okay?" I caught a whiff of the chili and a hint of Helen's gardenia perfume, a mix of sweet and spicy.

She quickly arranged all her supplies, her large bangle bracelets clanking together as she worked. A moment or two later, she was on her way, leaving me to return to the stillness of my store. It seemed everyone had someplace else to be. Old Port Passage Way, our main island road, was almost empty and it was a little disturbing. If you had asked me, I probably would have told you I was simply enjoying a peaceful day.

But the truth was, I wasn't fully ready for the post-busy season quiet. The build-up of having community events, crowded ferry boats,

and unexpectedly rented island accommodations allowed me to post-
pone thinking about my upcoming quieter months. Even after all the
fun and energy of last night's social event, I found myself restless and
unsettled today, feeling like something was coming. This was my first
glimpse at a slower pace, revealing itself at the very brink of a new
season, presenting me with new uncertainty. Maybe Barb was right
that this quiet and calm was exactly what I needed to move forward
in an intentional, focused way. But in reality, I would have welcomed
a distraction of any kind.

Was I ready to face this next phase of my Mongin Island journey?
Would life always be like this now? I didn't remember questioning
myself this much as a new parent, a new wife, or a new professional.
Now, where everything was concurrently familiar and still brand new,
I could only admit that I saw these seasons, still, as something I had
to get through. Time to get busy doing something, I decided. I needed
a project I could balance with the coming slower, seasonal pace.

It was cloudy Monday afternoon when the bell tinkled and
announced the arrival of Annabelle, Tracy, and Mary Frances, who
each wanted a paperback for their spa day.

"Hot stone massages and facials are our only agenda items for the
afternoon," Tracy announced, "Well, maybe we can add a specialty
drink from Treehouse Coffee on the ride back."

"Now, that's an agenda I could get behind!" I agreed as I rang up
their totals.

"Carrie will be sorry she missed this," Annabelle said softly to Mary
Frances.

But Tracy snapped in response, her small lips tightening into a
thin line, "I wouldn't be so sure of that, Annabelle. She made that
crystal clear last night. Absolutely nothing was going to get in the
way of her date today. She was taking the boat to the mainland, having lunch, and all of it was none of our business. Remember? She told
you specifically that she hoped she would be gone all day, and for us
to stay out of it with any commentary. Doesn't sound like she is going
to be missing our spa day, does it?"

Tracy looked at me for confirmation. "Well, it sounds like you all have some things planned that you will enjoy," I answered without really answering.

"Well, it's just that—" she started.

"Let's see if we can check in early at the spa and maybe see what the 'lavender calming room' is all about," Mary Frances chimed in. I noticed the quick eyeroll shared between her and Annabelle as I handed them their purchases. "We could all do with some relaxation and a perspective shift. See you later, Carr!"

Before too long, it was time for my first Book Buddy event. A few island children started arriving, some having been dropped off by the small school bus that rattled along our island roads. "Hi friends! Come get settled in the Trading Floor!"

Soon the room was filled with backpacks. A couple of pairs of shoes were already piled in the corner near the squishy cushions I brought from my Atlanta home. It made me happy to see how comfortable these children were in this store and with each other. A few parents were chatting in the room, and one or two had grabbed a seat on the porch. Remarkably, no one had touched the plate of brownies or pitcher of lemonade arranged in the middle of the farm table.

"Hi, Miss Carr, I have a book to trade, and I packed it in my backpack. Can I pick a new one?"

"Jacob, I was looking for you. I baked some of your favorite chocolate chip brownies. Yes, of course, find what you like. Hi Katie, great to see you!" I greeted Jacob and his mom.

Although her housekeeping job at the resort was physically demanding, and she was balancing her work and her role as Jacob's sole parent, the dark circles that lined her eyes when I first met her months ago were long gone. Maybe it helped to have a consistent schedule or the safety and support of this community—whatever it was, Katie looked happy, relaxed, and confident. She had found her rhythm as Jacob's mom.

"Carr, thanks for hosting this event for the children. Jacob is so excited to read to Buddy, he has been talking about it since you posted it on your website. Did you know he invited a friend from his class to join us today? That's a big step for him."

"We talked about doing this over the summer, and Jacob's enthusiasm for it has been very motivating. I think Buddy is just as excited, I told him he needed to have his listening ears ready." We laughed together.

As if on cue, Buddy wandered into the room. First, he greeted his "fan club". Then he settled on one of the cushions. There were plenty of pets, head pats, and tummy rubs to go around, everyone had some kind of greeting for this dog. Buddy responded with his usual tail wagging and a couple of quick kisses on cheeks, chins, and hands. How anyone could have ever abandoned this dog will forever be a mystery to me.

"Friends, after your snack, if you haven't brought a book with you, please find one here that interests you. Mr. Tripp has pulled a few things he thought you might like. When it's your turn, you can read a few pages to Buddy, and the rest of us will follow along. When you're done, let us know if we can ask you a few questions about the story or if you are ready for it to be someone else's turn. Remember, Buddy has been waiting for you to tell him these stories, it has been a long time since someone read aloud to him. He is very excited to hear from you all. Also, Buddy doesn't mind if you need to take a break and sound out words or if you need to start over. He is just happy to hear the story you pick. Who wants to go first?"

The energy in the room settled, and the children quickly became an attentive audience for all the readers, some who struggled and some who breezed through their selection. None of that mattered. They all enjoyed petting Buddy distractedly as they read. Some even curled up with him on the cushion and held his paw with one hand and their book with another. I wanted to freeze this moment forever.

"I was going to snap a few pictures of our superstars here and post them on our events page," Tripp said quietly to me, and then using his best teacher voice, he announced, "Hey, excuse me, before Addison starts her Amelia Bedelia chapter, can we all circle around so I can get some photos of our very first Book Buddy group?"

There was shuffling, laughing, readjustments, and opinions that needed to be sorted out. Tripp had it all under control, so I went to meet and greet my customers. Books & Brew was bustling, filled with shoppers and readers. I noticed every rocker on the porch was occupied with people reading or visiting and I was instantly energized. So much for worrying about a slower pace. That would be a care for another day.

"You must be the infamous Carr. Everywhere we go, I'm told you are the person I need to meet." I turned, almost bumping into a petite woman whose almond brown eyes crinkled into her broad smile. "I'm Poppy Haveril, and you have quite the Mongin Island following!"

"I was hoping to meet you. Barb told me about your arrival, and I am so happy you will be with us for the next few weeks. Welcome to Books & Brew!"

"A much-needed addition, I will tell you that." She smiled as she took the room in. "Your aesthetic is really on point, it's welcoming and cozy here. Love the balance between the tall shelves and the tall windows, very good harmony."

"That is high praise, thank you! Have you been settling in well? I heard you are staying at the house right near the Inn on the resort property. What a view you must have!"

"Incredible water view, right to the mainland with the sea birds landing on the beach. It is quite the place for dreaming and creating. I design fabrics and silk prints, so this house has not only been inspirational for my husband's painting, but for my work as well. We settled in nicely, thank you. We spent the last few days organizing our spaces and figuring out the light patterns, and all the tasks of setting up shop. However, now it is time to start poking our heads out of our shells, like the turtles nesting on Rosemont Beach. No matter how many weeks we plan to stay, it is never long enough."

"I understand you are regular visitors to the island. Do you always rent the same place?"

"Many times, yes, we rent this exact house. It suits us so well. We have done it enough times now, we almost come to think of it as ours." She smiled softly and continued. "Granted, we have tried out a few other places as well, several were not as close to the beach. This one is our favorite, all the windows give us views from almost every room. Looking at the beach and all those beautiful trees, nothing makes me feel more at home."

We spent a few more minutes getting to know each other better. Poppy and Dan had many travel adventures that inspired their work. Their semi-nomadic life, a result of their projects and commissioned work, was their foundation of tidbits and stories—I could have listened to her for hours. We agreed to grab coffee in the next week or two. Her voice bubbled over the words as she spoke, almost like she was painting a story right before me. I was mesmerized. But the store was crowded, and it was time for me to focus on some of the tasks at hand. My daydreaming would have to wait. After pointing her to the memoir shelf she inquired about, I tidied up a few misplaced books and went to check in with the customers on the front porch.

I recognized a few of Helen's book club members, who were lined up next to each other in the rockers. Each held a cool drink, notebook, journal, or small computer tablet on their lap.

"Have I interrupted an impromptu meeting of your book club?" I asked the group.

"Not at all," Joyce said quickly. Her role as 'Helen's second in command' was firmly established. "We are working our way through the list of book possibilities for our next three meetings—enough to get us through the end of the year."

"If I can help you by ordering your selections, just let me know."

"Well, we have been a little distracted in our discussions and haven't made much progress," Julia said. "I guess there was a situation at the ferry landing earlier, and well, I wouldn't call it gossiping but …"

"It's not gossip, Julia, to state facts. That's all I was doing, I was just stating what I saw."

"Well, you might as well tell Carr what it was. Now we're just being rude, talking about this while she has no idea what we are referring to." Helen almost scolded as she uncrossed and recrossed her legs in front of her, the tips of her shoes barely touching the porch. "Go ahead, Joyce, finish what you started."

I felt as if I had walked into a conversation that no one wanted to have, but concurrently it also seemed like a discussion everyone wanted to have—I hated things like this.

"It's not that big of a deal, the drama just was a sight, I tell you. I was simply saying that it will be nice when things quiet down." Joyce began, settling into her chair, straightening her back, and putting a hand on each armrest. As she began her story, she rocked a little faster.

"One of our visitors was really calling out her companion. I couldn't quite hear the specifics, but I heard the loud voices and saw a lot of pointing and arms waving. As the lady who was boarding the boat tried to walk down the gangway, the other lady even tried to grab her arm. I mean yelling and shouting, causing a scene. The poor thing almost fell right into the marsh grass growing near the shore. She steadied herself and practically ran the rest of the way—like she was trying to get away from the other lady. I tell you, it was quite a spectacle. It's a good thing the boat passenger was traveling light. If she had a duffle or backpack, I am sure she would have lost her balance and likely would have gone for an unexpected swim."

"It's so strange," Julia agreed. "We don't usually see people running down the dock, unless, of course, they are late to board the boat."

Helen jumped in, "Well, that's not what this was, right? We all know that. Maybe it's the summer heat making people short-tempered, but whatever it is, I am ready for cooler and quieter days. I'm at the end of my rope with other people's nonsense spilling into our way of life." Her fuse was short with everyone and almost all of us had some kind of nonsense, according to her. Even her closest friends weren't spared her sharp tone lately.

Reluctantly, I asked Joyce to describe what these women at the ferry looked like, although I already felt like I could have reasonably guessed the answer. Joyce described Tracy and Carrie perfectly.

Chapter 4

"Is that mine or yours?" Barb asked as she dug through the nylon backpack at her feet, looking for her cell phone.

I love it when she stops by at the end of her workday. We were tucked into my office, sharing tastes of several new tea selections. In the sample box I received Monday was a pumpkin chai and something delightful called Autumn Mist. It was a green tea combined with tangy apples and rose hips flavors. The hardest part, so far, was deciding which one to offer the customers first. To Barb, it seemed not quite "fall enough" for pumpkin anything, and she was making a good case for waiting until cooler weather to start brewing the chai.

"I think it's yours. Mine must be on the front counter by the register. I don't see it here." I shifted some papers around on my desk but came up empty-handed.

She kept digging until she announced, "What is happening? I've got four missed calls and ten notifications! How did I miss all this?" Her forehead crinkled with concern. She scrolled quickly and then put the phone to her ear as she listened to her voicemail messages.

"You know, the reception stinks back here, I missed a few ..." I started to say.

Barb stood up and blurted, "I have to go, I have to get over to the resort. Something's happened. I can't make heads or tails out of this."

We looked at each other, saying it all, without saying a word. It had only been a few months since Carl's death. Losing our neighbor and friend and helping Deputy Julie with her case was still a not-so-distant memory.

"Let me see if Tripp will watch the store, I'll come with you." Whatever she was facing, I didn't want her to be alone.

With Buddy and Books & Brew in Tripp's expert hands, Barb quickly turned her golf cart around and pulled onto Old Port Passage Way before she explained, "It was Mary Frances, you know, from the girls' trip?"

"What's happened? What did she say?" I prompted her.

"Maybe it's nothing, it's probably nothing. Right?" She looked at me, hopeful. But then she shook her head slightly and continued, "It doesn't feel like nothing. It feels like she is concerned but trying not to sound concerned. You know what I mean?"

She took a deep breath and continued, "The messages don't make sense. I think she is asking for help finding one of her friends, it sounds like someone is missing. I can't really tell what she is asking. I think she is saying that Carrie might be missing."

"Missing? What do you mean missing? What did she say specifically?"

"She asked me if I knew where someone could hide on the island, and then in the next message, she asked if I could help her get people to look for someone who was hiding. The last one is where she mentions Carrie. It's a jumbled mess. I am wondering if the messages were delivered out of order."

"People? Like our neighbors? Mary Frances thinks one of her friends is playing a game and hiding? I am so confused by this. Who is missing? Did she for sure say Carrie was gone?" I searched Barb's face as she expertly drove around the potholes at the edge of the resort driveway. We were nearly there.

"It's probably some kind of misunderstanding. Those four aren't on the same page. Maybe one of them just needs space, and just wants some alone time." I tried to reason away the doom I was feeling.

Barb handed me her phone and said, "Look at the texts that came in, and if you can hear well enough, go ahead and play the voicemails. The last one is hands down the strangest message I think I've ever got. Has Mary Frances looked around this island? Someone could be hiding almost anywhere. The woods are dense, the roads are quiet, and many places are off the beaten path. This someone, maybe Carrie, could be anywhere. Of course, I know places people could hide. What kind of a question is that? Just by looking around everyone would know that. It's weird, right?"

"Hiding from what?" I asked, reading the messages quickly. "Mary Frances texted that they haven't seen Carrie since early this morning—she is definitely talking about Carrie. Why do they think she is hiding instead of just needing some distance from them? Hiding is an odd word choice, I agree."

I was asking questions neither of us could answer. Still, saying them aloud prepared us both for asking better questions when we were with Mary Frances and her friends. The urgency in Mary Frances' voice and the repeated messages made this feel heavy to us both. There was a hint of controlled panic that was not lost on either of us.

The Rosemont Resort's central location on our small island meant everything else was only a short golf cart ride away from its beautiful, historic sixty-room Inn, beach cottages, restaurants, and all the other amenities. We were soon cruising to the center of the resort and arrived at the row of oceanfront beach cottages in just a minute or two. Barb sat on the edge of the cart's bench seat, and her leg stretched to push the accelerator down to the floorboard. We quickly zoomed under the canopy of the old oak trees lining the main street of the property.

"This woman could be anywhere, just on the resort property alone. Right? If Carrie is hiding, she could hide forever." Barb made a sharp left turn and quickly parked her cart in front of the largest cottage.

It had an open-concept floor plan, and its spacious family room was framed with windows that faced the ocean. From the pine-needle-covered lawn, we could see Mary Frances, Annabelle, and Tracy standing around the kitchen island.

"Ready for this?" Barb asked as she locked the cart's parking brake into place.

"Let's see if we can help sort this out. Between the two of us, we know the island well and maybe can think of some spots Carrie may go if she wanted some peace and quiet."

Tracy opened the navy-blue front door before we could knock. "Thank you for coming, Barb. We just aren't sure what to do. Hi Carr, sorry to bother you with this. Come in, please." She swung the door open and stepped to the side to let us pass. When the door was firmly closed behind us, she wrapped her arms around herself protectively.

We walked into a scene that competed with the breezy vacation personas we met at Books & Brew, the Chili Cook-Off, and the resort spa. Open cabinets and drawers, dirty dishes piled on the kitchen surfaces, shoes, and discarded clothing creating trails to the different bedrooms made it hard to focus on any one thing. Stuff was jumbled, piled, and thrown in every available spot. This cottage was a chaotic mess.

"Wow …" Barb said under her breath as she looked around. Knowing Barb, the idea of preparing this cottage for the next guest immediately weighed heavily on her.

We joined them at the granite kitchen island and mugs of coffee appeared in front of us. "So, what's going on? Carrie seems to be hiding, you said. How can we help?" I asked as Barb and I settled into the tall woven stools that lined the island while the three of them remained standing.

Annabelle answered immediately, "This trip is a disaster. Everything about it. I can't wait to leave and just so you know, I am not doing this again. I am not, so don't ask me."

"No one forced you to come, that's for sure, and no one will force you on another trip," Tracy snapped.

"If, maybe, you weren't on Carrie every single minute of every single day maybe, just maybe we wouldn't be sitting here trying to figure out what is actually happening, right? Maybe if we could have just gone on a trip and just let everyone enjoy it, we wouldn't now have to spend our day trying to find Carrie and woo her back." The two of them glared at each other, gatekeeping the other words that seemed to be bubbling up, near the surface of exploding into the room.

"My immediate concern is that in just a few hours, it will be dark, and we have no idea where Carrie is. Our golf cart is here, so we know she didn't take that, and it looks like most of her stuff is here." Mary Frances shifted the conversation.

"So, you woke up today, and then what?" I prompted.

"When I got up, I made some coffee and noticed that Carrie's bedroom door was open. I went to close it so I wouldn't disturb her as I started breakfast. I saw that her bed was empty. When I pushed open the door, I saw her bathroom door was also open. She was not in her room, I thought she went for a beach walk or whatever. She hasn't returned, her phone is off, calls go right to voicemail, and texts aren't delivered. We have already walked the beach, been to the resort restaurants, and gone to all the places within walking distance. I don't know what else to do at this point," Mary Frances answered for the group.

"It's been all day," Annabelle emphasized.

"What time was it when you saw her last? Can you say for sure that she has been gone since this morning?" I asked.

Tracy said quietly, "We got into an argument last night. We were watching a movie and she got up to sit on the screened porch. Alone. That's when things went downhill fast."

"They went downhill because you wouldn't stop, Tracy," Annabelle shouted. "Yes, Carrie has been short-tempered and not like herself, we all agree on that, but you added fuel to that fire. You just would not stop." Her fist thumped the kitchen island with each word of her last sentence.

"It's just that—" Tracy began, but Mary Frances raised her voice over them both.

"Regardless of who said what to whom, regardless of any of it, Carrie is gone. We have looked, we have called, we split up and went to all the logical places. I want to say that she is hiding since she is likely as frustrated with us as we are frustrated with her." She took a deep breath, smoothed her hands down her red capri pants, and then began again, clearly in command of the room.

She turned toward her friends and said, "Tracy, you said you peeked into her room during the night because you wanted to apologize to her. Is that right?"

Tracy's eyes were glued to the counter in front of her, "Yes, I feel terrible. Yes, I wanted to apologize. I thought maybe we could go for a walk today to talk it all out. Last night, I knocked on her door, she didn't answer but her bathroom light was on. I waited in the kitchen for a few minutes. After that, I gave up and went to bed. Thought I'd catch her this morning. I hate that we fought all week." I could barely hear Tracy's voice above the hum of the dishwasher.

"Carrie may have started it but now it's been you, Tracy, pointing out all the wrong things. Carrie barely said anything to us yesterday, nothing of any real meaning," Annabelle immediately chimed in.

I jumped in before we looped around it all again. The circle of blame and accusation was providing nothing useful. "Just to be clear, you didn't actually see Carrie again after y'all called it a night. You didn't put your eyes on her, right? The last time you physically saw her was earlier last night. True?"

"True," Mary Frances agreed. By the look that crossed her face, I could tell she now understood this could be more than Carrie "hiding". Annabelle and Tracy nodded their heads, and there was a shift in the room's vibe.

I have often thought about moments like this, the times when one or two simple words convey more than paragraphs strung together and when the power of a few words, said plainly and decisively, changes the course of a conversation. The snapshots in my memory, where I was, who I was with, and what the room felt like are so vivid because of one or two words were said so impactfully, that I have not been able to let them go. This felt like one of these times.

Choosing my words gently, I said, "This feels like we may need more help than what Barb and I can provide. Of course, we will search, just as you did. And we know quite a few neighbors who will definitely join us. There are many good people here who will answer your call for help. But I am not sure that is the only thing you need right now. Do you want me to call the sheriff's department and get some guidance?"

"Do you really think that is necessary? I mean, I think Carrie wants to—" Tracy began.

"We do," Barb cut her off. "At the minimum, the sheriff or deputy can give us an idea of the best way to search the walkable areas on the resort property. It's so dense with the woods and the undeveloped land. We don't know what Carrie was wearing, or what her plans were, and we don't know that she didn't accept a ride that may have been offered to her. We don't have a lot to go on and as you say, we only have a few hours until it's dark. You know, during turtle nesting season especially, there are minimal exterior lights on, and residents with homes facing the beach are asked to be careful with interior lights, so the area surrounding these cottages will be pitch dark in just a few hours. We need to use the time we have wisely."

It was decided. Barb was tasked with calling several neighbors who would help search and who would spread the word for more volunteers. She directed Annabelle, Tracy, and Mary Frances to each go back to a different resort hotspot and share a picture of Carrie. Since they had recent photos on their phones, they could help the staff recognize Carrie and remember if they had seen her during the day.

For my part, I decided I would call Deputy Julie, since she had law enforcement responsibility for Mongin Island. My work with her to solve the case of Coastal Carl's death a few months ago solidified our relationship. She would point me in the right direction.

Chapter 5

"What in the world?" Julie cut me off a few minutes into my summary of the new situation in which we found ourselves. "Hiding? Who says a grown woman is hiding? Adults don't normally hide unless they are in danger. Do you think Carrie thought she was in danger?"

"I can't imagine what danger she perceived. Annoyed—yes, frustrated—yes, and maybe even bored—yes, I will give you all that. But in danger, well, I can't really say. I barely know her, the woman said a handful of words to me. I can't tell you that, but I agree, 'hiding' struck the wrong chord with me, too."

"There is no truth to the myth of waiting twenty-four hours before determining someone is officially missing. I think that's a leftover from Hollywood. People may like to wait for tempers to settle down, and emotions to quiet. People often return on their own when cooler heads prevail. Since we aren't sure when she left, and we don't have a lot of information, I am going to authorize opening a missing persons case for Carrie. Given the island landscape and the fact that she is a visitor who doesn't know her way around well, I think it is in her best interest if we don't wait—the first twelve to twenty-four hours are critical. Let's do this."

Within the hour, Julie and her team met us at the beach cottages. The neighbors Barb had organized showed up just as we thought they would. Deputy Julie and Lieutenant Cole had set up a makeshift command center in the cottage family room and more law enforcement help was arriving, adding technology and resources.

Even though this was the resort's largest rental unit, it still was not big enough to contain all the coming and going of the team working to find Carrie. Someone had cleared all the clutter, clothes, and assorted remnants Carrie, Mary Frances, Tracy, and Annabelle had casually discarded. In their place were computers, whiteboards, and other tools. The family room we had just been in was almost unrecognizable.

"Carr, Barb, this is Commander Fresio. He is the incident commander and will keep us on track here." Deputy Julie introduced us to the tall, bald officer seated at the center of a folding table, now this room's focal point. There were two other tables, one on each side of him, that created a U-shaped hub. His stature and presence filled the room.

"Thank you for coming so quickly, how can we help?" I shook his strong hand.

He answered without hesitation, "Two things, right off the bat. First, let's make sure we have all the details of the last few hours with Miss Carrie. You can provide any information you have to Lieutenant Basco, seated behind me. Tameka, these two volunteers will be over to see you in a minute." He called to Lieutenant Basco, stationed at the kitchen island. She appeared to be listening intently to someone speaking into her headset. She looked up and nodded but continued her work.

"And next, in the last few hours of light, your biggest help will be organizing the volunteers you called. I identified six key points on the map on the board over there. Those spots are a priority right now based on their walkable proximity to this cottage." He pointed to the large whiteboard that now blocked the beautiful windows we had looked through when we first arrived. "How about you work with Julie to assign a group to each of those areas? Pick an area leader, and then you can help collect the information the volunteers provide. We will have officers working through the data and the resort has offered several of their non-essential employees. There will be a lot of boots on the ground. Julie will take the lead, but you can help direct the people you brought. Sound good?"

"Yes, we are on it," Barb quickly agreed. The commander had already dismissed us, reverting his attention to the screens in front of him.

We shared what little we knew with Lieutenant Basco, who listened and typed as we spoke. She nodded encouragingly and tilted her head to the left as if she were facilitating the words to travel from our lips to her ears. When we paused, she asked, "Is that everything?"

"Yes, like we said, we just got a call to—" Barb began.

"Well, thank you. And take this card, it has the command center phone number. It is faster if you call this number and keep us informed." We were dismissed again.

From the small front deck of the cottage, we could see the crowd of volunteers had already doubled in size. We knew we needed to get to work quickly, and the commander was right, the community was ready to help. Deputy Julie handed us a stack of Carrie's pictures for us to distribute and then she addressed the crowd.

"We are asking you to search one of six areas. We are going to do this in an organized way. Please take a card and a photo. We are looking for a Caucasian woman, 41 years old, with long, straight blonde hair. Carrie sometimes wears glasses. She is of medium build, approximately 5'9" tall. She has no distinguishing tattoos, piercings, or scars. We don't know what she was last wearing so please take a good look at the picture. Use the number on the card to call the command center, and relay any tips, observations, concerns, or comments. One of our officers will direct you. Thank you all for your work here tonight. Let's meet back here at 8:00 p.m. and we will have a plan for tomorrow, if needed. Thank you, everyone."

We quickly split up and I joined the group assigned to search the beach in front of the cottages, the dense dunes, and the area around the beach club, where the casual dining restaurant was nestled at the end of the resort property. Rosemont Beach had miles of powdery sand, some small dunes, and lots of marsh grass. The area behind the beach club melted into another neighborhood. We worked silently and diligently until it was time to head back to the command center. The low tide offered us the widest beach to explore, but the sun was quickly sinking, and it was nearly dark. Our search was over, for now.

The volunteers' faces were noticeably imprinted with the strain of the last few hours. We had not received any communication from Deputy Julie or Commander Fresio indicating that Carrie had been found, and as volunteers began to gather in front of the cottages, the crowd was quiet and a little lost. I guessed we weren't the only ones who had expected to locate Carrie and had anticipated this gathering would be turning into a celebration.

"Thank you all for your help," Commander Fresio spoke above the volunteers' buzz. "We will continue our work tomorrow morning at first light. If you can spare some time and want to continue to assist us, we will gather in this spot at 7:00 a.m. and begin our search at 7:15 a.m. Team leads, please provide your data summaries to the officers located near Deputy Julie's black Suburban." Almost before his last word was spoken, he evaporated into the cottage, leaving our unanswered questions, thoughts, and comments to circulate amongst ourselves.

We walked in weighted silence to Barb's cart. This scene all seemed too soon, too heavy. Barb spoke first, "It's unbelievable to me. How does this happen? They just got here; how does Carrie go missing on an island that is only a few miles long? I can't remember anyone being missing, ever. Where is she?"

We didn't speak the rest of the short way back to my house. "You up for this tomorrow?" I asked Barb as I climbed out and looked up at my own family room windows. I could see Buddy's sweet face waiting to greet me. Tripp had returned him home and turned on all my usual lights, welcoming me to my own safe space.

"I have a few hours I can spend in the morning, yes, want me to pick you up?"

"Tripp already texted to say he would watch the store even though it is supposed to be his day off. That man, he would give the shirt off his back for this island. Thanks for the ride, see you around 7:00."

As I closed the door behind me and greeted Buddy, who wiggled and wagged with joy, I knew tonight needed to be an early night—tomorrow was likely going to be a very long day.

Chapter 6

Word had spread by next morning and the community of both residents and tourists responded—volunteers lined the street in front of the cottages. People were ready to help, and they were serious, focused, and waiting for direction, knowing they soon would be assigned important work.

In front of the cottages, under the tall oaks and pine trees, there was a table set up with a breakfast spread and I noticed Miss Lucy, the island's unofficial baker, unpacking an oversized seagrass basket filled with golden brown muffins.

"These are my Morning Glories, got a couple of dozen here. Hoping they give y'all a boost. Come, have a cup of this new blend from Treehouse Coffee, they brewed something wonderful from their store for all of us." Miss Lucy was efficient in everything she did—she answered my question before I even asked.

As I got closer, I could see that "a couple dozen" of these beauties was an understatement. Hidden under the table were Miss Lucy's travel bakery containers filled with these apple spice and carrot cake treats. As usual, she took care of her community in her own quiet way.

"You outdid yourself, once again. We likely will need some fuel today, there is certainly a lot of searching to do. Thank you for all this."

I pointed to her table and the goods stashed beneath the chambray tablecloth.

Her dark eyes measured me. "Are you ready for what is in front of us?" she asked, dismissing the compliment with her signature modesty.

"Has something else happened? Is there news?" I answered, searching her face for some clue, but she had years of keeping the things people shared with her to herself.

"Girl, these old bones, they feel the things the island tells us. Today will be a day we will remember." That was as much as she was going to give me, she would say no more. Her attention shifted as she greeted several volunteers, offering them her baked goods or a cup of coffee. Miss Lucy's talent was legendary on the island and there was soon a small line waiting for one of her treats. I turned toward the cottage, empty-handed. My earlier optimism that this would be the day we brought Carrie home was replaced with dread—I was no longer hungry.

Neighbors and guests stood together, but the air was heavy with anticipation and ambiguity. Bits of softly voiced concerns reached me. How could Carrie go missing on this island? It was exactly as Barb had said last night—no one goes missing here. Everyone has a place on Mongin Island, and we keep our eyes out for each other. How did this happen?

My thought had me traveling down several different roads, but I was jolted back to this moment when the cottage door was thrown open, and officers went in a dozen directions at once. Some jumped in nearby cars, golf carts, or all-terrain vehicles. A few more ran toward the beach, heading down past the Rosemont Inn. The crowd froze as we tried to absorb what was happening, and the almost-whispered conversations ended immediately as we watched something significant begin to unfold.

Last out the door was Mary Frances. With wide eyes, she scanned the crowd, but her face showed no sign of recognizing what she was seeking. Her arms were tucked into a long, gray cardigan sweater but underneath were the same clothes she was wearing yesterday. I wondered if she had slept.

"Mary Frances, what can we do to help?" I approached her gently.

Her eyes slowly focused on my face, and I watched them fill. "Carrie, it's Carrie. I know it is. It has to be, right? It's Carrie ..." she broke off as I lightly rubbed her back.

Before I could ask more, Annabelle and Tracy were at her side and they were all connected, arms wrapped around shoulders and waists.

Annabelle spoke in almost a whisper, "Something has been found in the dune grass, on the other side of the Inn. The police have asked us to wait here, but ..."

"We think it's Carrie," Tracy finished her sentence.

Chapter 7

"You'll stay with them?" Julie asked as she took a few quick steps backward, toward her Suburban. The wind blew her long, thick, blonde curls over her face. She expertly gathered her hair with her right hand and pulled it into a tight ponytail with her left. There were a few ringlets that framed her face and bounced as she moved away from us.

She didn't wait for my answer, either because she already knew what I would say or because the urgency of the situation demanded her immediate attention. Mary Frances, Annabelle, Tracy, and I moved inside the cottage and waited. None of us knew exactly what we were waiting for, and if you had asked, we may all have had different answers to that question. The cottage was filled with sadness, shock, and the impact of words that likely should never have been said, things that could never be undone. We sat on different cushions of the neutral-colored sectional sofa, keeping our distance from each other, lost in our thoughts. Likely the only thing we shared in those moments was the utter disbelief of the circumstances. I am not sure how long we sat there, trying to patch together unfinished sentences and questions without answers.

Eventually, after preparing sandwiches that went uneaten and helping the officers pack up some equipment from the command center, I needed a little fresh air. Standing outside alone, where only a few hours ago the community gathered so hopefully, the emotions I had ignored while trying to support these women rose right to the surface. The tears came easily, and my hands shook with the release. My Mongin Island did not disappoint me—the ocean sounds and the smell of the cooler salt air all worked their usual magic. I gathered myself, ready now to attend to the messages and calls I had silenced.

After confirming that Buddy was with Tripp, and Barb had left the resort to attend to some work deadlines, I addressed Julie's "call me" text.

She answered on the first ring, "Can you make your way down to the Gateway Cottages? Leave the ladies and head down here. We are right past the blue cottage." The call ended without me saying a word. I assured Mary Frances, Tracy, and Annabelle I would return with more information soon. My heart broke for them. They seemed so lost.

Cutting through the center of the resort saved some steps. Moments later, I crossed the golf course fairway and walked diagonally to the white fence that guarded a small path leading to the Gateway Cottages. All these houses, each painted a different pastel color, faced the Atlantic and were built on tall wood pylons buried in the sand, which allowed the sea to wash underneath them at high tide. They looked like giant gumdrops dotted along the white sand. Julie left the group of officers and met me at the gateway.

"You walked?" Julie asked as she came to meet me at the path.

"I rode with Barb earlier today, she has the cart. Got here as fast as I could."

"This is not official, but, well, Carrie has been found. The Loggerhead Turtle Patrol was out checking their nests on this side of the resort early this morning and unfortunately, they found Carrie lying on her side. Way up there, hidden in the dune grass. You know, during turtle hatching, no one really goes through the dunes and marsh grass. They just happened to stumble upon her, right near a nest. Identification will be forthcoming, of course, but well, there it is."

"Her friends will be devastated. This is just surreal," I said, replaying her words in my mind to absorb them. "Can you tell me what happened? What do we say to them?"

"That's the thing. There is no obvious trauma to the victim. I can't answer that for you. Maybe some kind of medical emergency, but that's just a guess, of course. I thought you—"

I interrupted, unintentionally, "Why do you think she was lying on her side?"

Julie half-smiled at me. "You really don't miss a trick, do you? Not sure about lying on her side, actually. It's not normally how we find victims for sure. Without knowing the cause of death, it's hard to say. Could be that she was positioned that way by someone. Keep in mind though, that bodies can move after death, did you know that?"

Julie could tell by my expression that I did not, in fact, know that. She continued, "Post-mortem movements are usually appendage positional changes, but in some rare cases ..." she broke off, looking vaguely at the ocean in front of us, searching for the right words. "We will know more in a few hours after the medical examiner has completed his work," she finished quietly.

She took a deep breath and continued, "Carr, I want to get this right this time. I wasn't straightforward with you when it came to investigating Coastal Carl's death. I am going to need someone here on the island to help. I don't want there to be any misunderstanding between us, I am asking for your help—there is a lot of ground to cover. Since I am a boat ride away, we both know it's not the same as being here all day and from what I can gather, Carrie didn't just stay here on the island. There could be lots of different theories that need to be explored. Are you willing?"

"You know what I am going to say, right?" I looked at her and then slowly, softly smiled.

"You're going to tell me you don't know how you can be of any help to me. But then you will say you will do it for the island, to help your community feel safe and be at peace again. You will do it because the island has helped you and now the island needs help. Am I right?"

"Am I really that predictable?" I paused, then decided. "I will help you, although I am not sure exactly what to do."

"I have some ideas. My team will finish up here, I think they are about done with the turtle team, but they will process the scene here. Let's go to the cottage and talk to the women there. After that, your biggest help will be with talking to people to learn more about what they saw, what they know—you are likely one of the few people on the island who actually spent any time with the victim."

The plan was set, and the difficult news was delivered as gently as possible. It was poorly received. The three women had completely different reactions. Mary Frances crumbled on the sofa, crying fresh tears. Annabelle questioned and probed for details we did not yet have, almost suggesting the lack of concrete answers could leave the door open for us to have the wrong victim. And Tracy stood with her arms crossed, saying nothing, showing nothing, and offering nothing. She abruptly went to her bedroom and closed the door behind her. We left moments later and were on our way to Books & Brew.

Julie broke the silence, "Kind of a lot, right? Is that what you are thinking?"

I agreed; it was a lot—the emotion, the details, the things that were said with and without words. I tried my best to absorb them all while not getting lost.

In just a few minutes, wheels crunched the parking lot's tabby shells, and we worked out the framework of our plan surprisingly quickly. Julie would focus on shepherding the forensic details through all the right processes, and I would gather information that would help understand Carrie's movements over the last few days. As needed, we would widen our circle of things to investigate. We both agreed we had a long list of conversations to have, places to explore, and information to find.

"Do you want to come in, have something to eat or drink, before you head back to the mainland?" I asked as I hopped down. Customers were gathered on the front porch, rockers were moving at different speeds. Was it my imagination that everyone's pace slowed when they saw Deputy Julie's car?

Julie did not take me up on my offer for any refreshments. We were both ready to get started trying to understand the latest Mongin Island mystery.

Chapter 8

It was so reassuring to walk into Books & Brew and see everything exactly as it should be. The reclaimed wood floor reflected the light from the wall of windows, the new inventory had already been added to the tall wooden shelves that lined the room, and the oil-rubbed bronze chandeliers that hung in the center of each room helped the store glow. Tripp was helping some customers in the local author section. Buddy was curled up in his chair and the room smelled like a blend of our new teas.

I could see the tip of Buddy's tail wag as I walked closer to him. This little fuzzy boy knew I needed his encouragement. Tripp and Buddy came to find me as I started up my office computer and cleared off a workspace on my desk. Buddy climbed into his Black Watch plaid dog bed, positioned next to a row of windows. This room had the store's best view of every season's Mongin beauty. At that point in September, the black-eyed Susans slowly claimed the store's side yard and were Buddy's background. As he settled in, I got the sense he wanted to hear the news, too.

"So, I think I am up to date on the latest. How are Carrie's friends?"

"Not good. It's all of it—you know shock, anger, disbelief, grief, all of it. I feel terrible for them, Tripp. They came for a fun vacation, and they are leaving without their friend. Unimaginable."

"It is unimaginable. Brings up the stuff we don't really think about. Or I guess, we don't like to think about. We both know this all too well. Julie has asked you to be part of this? I saw her drop you off so I'm guessing you're getting called into all the action again?"

"Julie wants some help talking to people and finding out Carrie's movements. We have a plan and that means going back to talk to all her friends again, which may feel like an intrusion for them. Julie is working on getting Carrie's cell phone data, but that will take some time. I know, on top of all of it, people feel sad about Carrie but it's scary not knowing what happened to her. Islanders are probably wondering about their own safety. We have to figure this out, and quickly. It's the mixed blessing of having an extended tourist season. There are a lot of folks who will want answers and want them soon."

"Carr, you aren't responsible for solving this, you aren't responsible for how everyone feels. You know that, right? Before you ask, yes, I am absolutely fine with helping out more in the store and doing whatever needs to be done. Don't worry about the schedule, I can hold down things here. Plus, you know how much I enjoy spending time with our Buddy. The only thing I am worried about is you. Please, go easy on yourself."

We locked eyes, and I could tell he meant every word. His concern was easy to read, as was his support. "I can't do this without your help. The store, Buddy, being a sounding board, all of it, even answering questions from our customers. Thank you, Tripp, for all you do."

"What's first? Back to the cottage?" Tripp shifted the conversation to the present details. He was always most comfortable with the facts, the plans, the tangible action items, not the feelings of it all.

"Well, funny enough, the first thing is asking you if I can borrow your cart. Barb picked me up this morning, and that already seems like it was days ago. Do you mind?"

After preparing a few questions, I was on my way back to the Rosemont Resort. I knew that once I got started, the words would likely flow, but I was struggling to find the way to start this conversation.

Annabelle was sitting on the cottage's weathered wooden deck front steps, holding a soda can in both hands. She was bent at the waist and her long, brown hair fell over her shoulders and covered her face. She did not look up as I pulled into the space in front of the cottage.

"Hey, Annabelle. I'm sorry to bother y'all. I wanted to check on you, find out if you needed anything, and I ..." I wasn't sure if she heard me or even knew it was me.

She looked up, and I saw her eyes rimmed in red, swollen with tears. Annabelle looked pale and exhausted, but when she focused on me, she put the can down next to her. Wiping her face with her gray sweatshirt sleeve, she sat up. "Mary Frances is making the calls to Carrie's family and trying to sort out the details, the plans. I don't know all of it, I just know she is on the phone."

I nodded my head, but she offered nothing else.

"Tell me about the last few days. I heard you all, I heard your frustration with how things were going. But now I would like to hear what you knew about Carrie's plans, who she was speaking with, and anything she shared with you." I sat on the step below her and leaned my back against the white railing.

She sighed, "I don't even know where to begin." We sat in silence, the space between us filled with the soft sound of the distant tide coming in on Rosemont Beach. "Wait, why are you asking me this? Why do you want to know this?" She jolted into being fully present with me and looked at me suspiciously as she guarded Carrie's privacy.

"Since Deputy Julie isn't on the island full time, I'm gathering some info for her while she works with medical professionals and processes some of the things she found earlier today." I recognized her fragility, and I hoped my vague answer would be enough for her to trust me. I wasn't sure she understood that this was a potential crime.

She sighed again, "It's a mess. It's all just, I don't even know how to describe it. We grew up together, basically. We've been friends for decades, through life's highs and lows. Good times, bad times, really awful times. Sometimes weeks, maybe months go by, and we don't all talk, but then something happens, and we pick right up. You know? Life is busy, work, kids, divorce, sickness, stuff—but we always come back to each other. We can always count on each other."

She pulled the windblown hairs away from her face and continued, "Through it all, we were real friends, real friends who sometimes are amazing to each other—showing up to listen and support. Showing up after the breakups or the diagnoses, but other times we are just raw and unfiltered and messy and well, I guess that's what we all have been this week. Tracy especially, but well, to be honest, I had my fair share of it, too."

Between the palm trees in front of this cottage, I could see the water and kept my eyes focused there as she spoke. When she paused, I said, "You are lucky, blessed really, to have people like this in your life. The people who know the real you, the perfectly imperfect you, and love you anyway. I'm sorry. I know this is a tremendous loss for you all."

"Carrie's dad died about six months ago after a short battle with cancer. I think losing him combined with some milestones for all of us made her want, more than anything, to have a companion for the next part of her life. She told me, on a few occasions, that she was not dying alone. The irony that she was the only one of us talking about mortality ... well, isn't that something to think about."

"Is that when the dating app activity started?"

"Not exactly 'started', she met people through these apps in the past. Things started heating up in the last month or so, as far as I know."

"Do you know anything about the people she was speaking with or where she went yesterday? Was she talking to different people?" I had a million more questions I wanted to ask, but I recognized the need to go slowly.

Annabelle seemed to think about it and then said, "Carrie was definitely talking to a few people but there was one man she was excited about and spoke to and texted ... a lot. I think developing that relationship was where she was spending her time and I'm pretty sure that was the lunch date yesterday. She didn't tell me much and

I didn't ask … trying to give her some space. I don't know … maybe
I should have asked more." She looked at me, I think trying to figure
out if I was judging her or believing her. I wanted to hear more so I
stayed silent.

After a minute she continued, "She did say that 'Charles' lived
only about fifteen miles from her, in Midtown, but you know, with
Atlanta traffic that could be a thirty-minute ride, or it could take over
two hours. He traveled to Savannah for work pretty regularly. I think
she thought it was a good omen that she could meet him while she
was here. Carrie had been in California for a new account over the
last few weeks so I don't think they met in person before now … I
probably should have asked more. I wonder if she thought I wasn't
interested in knowing about it … I thought she would just know …"
She broke off and I knew we had reached the end of what Annabelle
could offer me right now.

"Do you mind if I head inside? I want to check in with Tracy and
Mary Frances and …" She shrugged and shifted to let me pass. I left
her as I found her, bent over with her forearms resting on her knees.

Mary Frances and Tracy were at the kitchen island, exactly where
Barb and I had sat only a day ago.

"Carrie's family is devastated. To say they are shocked is the
understatement of a lifetime. I just hung up from her mother," Mary
Frances shared as I crossed the room to join them.

"That poor woman, to lose her husband and her daughter, it's a
heartache no one should know." I stood across from them, with the
island between us.

"You must be exhausted, and I know you still have a lot to sort
out. I'm helping Deputy Julie while she manages and processes the
things her team found today. Is there anything you can think of that
would be helpful to Julie, any pieces of conversations that you heard?
Anything at all?"

Mary Frances shook her head, "Carrie kept things to herself. I
asked her, and she gave vague answers about 'someday' … so I can't
help you. I can't think straight right now. All I know is I have to figure
out how to help Carrie's mother with the arrangements, and then

what to do with all the things in her condo, getting her car back to Atlanta. I have a lot on my mind, and yet, I still don't feel like I even understand what is happening." For the first time since I met her, she looked unsure of herself and fragile, like she could snap in half.

Tracy pushed her stool away from the counter and stood quickly. "Don't look at me. I am not going to be blamed for this. All I did was try to get her to act like a normal person, not a desperate teenager." She gathered her phone and the drink that was resting on a stone coaster and hurried to her room. The door firmly shut behind her. The room felt crowded with emotion, accusation, and resentment swirling around.

"I'm going to leave you so you can rest. Is there anything you need? Do you have something to eat tonight?"

"Thank you, the neighbors brought over meals and snacks, all kinds of things. Miss Lucy left some muffins. The island has taken good care of us."

I was not surprised to hear this. The island had once again rallied and wrapped its arms around those who grace its shores.

"Before I go, I wondered if I could take Carrie's computer with me. Deputy Julie has Carrie's phone, but I thought I may be able to poke around, maybe see if I can read her texts through the messenger app on her computer."

Tracy's door suddenly whooshed open and she silently went into Carrie's room. A minute later, she handed over her computer, charger, and a piece of paper. "Her password is there, it's all our initials, starting with Carrie's and the year we met." Before I could ask anything else, she returned to her room, with her door walling her off from us. Somehow, I was leaving with more questions than when I arrived.

Chapter 9

Eventually, Buddy and I arrived back home. This day felt like a marathon through a mud puddle. Word was out on the island and the rest of my afternoon at Books & Brew was filled with people stopping in for either a new book, an update on Carrie, or both. I was drained, physically and emotionally. I scrounged for something quick to eat, showered, and was soon sitting on my screened porch with a cup of peppermint tea. Time to see what I could learn about Carrie and her mystery men.

The password Tracy shared gave me immediate access to Carrie's messages. I scrolled through the long list of conversations listed on the app. There were dozens to explore, and many with recent activity. Something didn't feel right. Before I got too far, I needed to figure that out.

I was so deep in thought that I must have missed the knock on my side door because I was startled seeing Barb standing in the porch doorway.

"Sorry, sorry, I knocked and called your name from the kitchen, didn't mean to make you jump!" She must have heard my gasp.

"I just was off in my own world. Guess I'm a little more on edge than usual. Come, sit down, I'm glad you stopped in."

"Tripp told me Julie has you on duty again, so I wanted to let you know I am throwing my hat in the ring as your trusty sidekick. Looks like you are already knee-deep in it. What did I miss?"

I smiled at Barb's ability to get right to it. "Julie did ask me to help so I went to talk to Carrie's friends. They don't seem to know much, I didn't really get anything usable from them—except Carrie's computer."

Barb settled into the chair closest to the sofa and turned on the gas fireplace as I went to get us some snacks. We were going to need reinforcements for this conversation. I do my best thinking if I crunch on something salty. I returned with a bottle of wine and a bowl of pita chips.

Barb pulled her chair closer to the coffee table and poured the wine. "Bringing out the big guns I see, the blue bowl of chips. Alright, let's have it."

No other explanation was needed. She knew I had a head full of thoughts to sort. "So, I think something is off, but I don't know, maybe it's me. I think this is the hardest part of helping Julie with these cases. She has seen such a wide variety of human behavior and responses in crisis. She has a much better idea of what is just 'off' versus what is suspicious. I, meanwhile, well, I am finding I question everything."

"I bet this is what makes you good at this, you do question everything. Other people just accept what they hear or see. What seems off to you?"

"At first, I thought I would pop open the computer and read the messages on her messenger app, catch up on the conversations. I asked for the computer because I thought it could be a fast way to find out where Carrie had lunch and more information about her date and other people, she met through dating sites. That was my plan."

"Yes, that sounds good. The cell phone location and official cell tower pings might not come until later tomorrow, right?"

"I think so, but Julie said sometimes the signals on these barrier islands like Mongin get rerouted to other cell towers. Sometimes they have to analyze the paths and put the pieces together to get exact locations. That may slow things down. While we wait, I thought the messages may give us a starting point that Julie could later confirm."

Barb nodded and I continued, "When I opened Carrie's computer, it felt invasive and nosy reading her messages. I scanned the conversations, but there were a lot to sort through. We all knew she was glued to her phone for these past few days, but there it is, on the screen. Lots of conversations and lots of activity. I need to read these, I know. It makes sense and likely will help us know where to start, especially since her close friends seem to know next to nothing."

"But, if they had her computer and Tracy had the password, then why didn't she already read her messages and tell us where Carrie went to lunch, or the name of the person she was meeting? Why not read them? Or, had Tracy already read them? Why does Tracy have Carrie's password? They don't live together or anywhere near each other—it's not like they shared this computer. Why does she know this? And why didn't she offer anything from these messages? Wouldn't that have been the very first thing you would have done if your dear friend was missing?"

Barb put her almost empty wine glass down and answered, "Something *is* off, I agree. Maybe it's—"

"And Annabelle was on the defensive about me asking questions, which also seemed a little odd," I interrupted Barb. "I would think they would care more about figuring out how she ended up dead on the Rosemont Inn beach."

I continued, "They all talk about 'giving Carrie space' but if your friend is missing, the island community is searching for her, and the police set up a command center—in your house—wouldn't you turn over every stone so she would have the best chance of being found? At the heart of it, at first, I thought I just was feeling uneasy about reading Carrie's private messages. I think my issue ultimately is either they already read the messages and didn't want to offer the information they found *or* they didn't read anything and left it to the police to figure out. Either way, something is weird."

We looked at each other and suddenly I was chilled, even though the fireplace was doing a decent job of pumping out some heat on this crisp evening.

"We are going to need more chips." Barb left to refill the bowl. Knowing her, she wanted a minute to process.

I watched the fire and waited. "You've stumped me on this one, I have to say. I can't come up with a scenario of how their actions make sense," she announced as she returned. "I agree, if Carrie's behavior bothered Tracy so much, it wouldn't be out of the realm of possibility that she would have snooped on her computer—even before Carrie went missing."

Knowing we were on the same page made the task at hand easier. We dug into Carrie's messages, with Barb taking notes as I read aloud, and we were through the layers of the most recent conversations in no time.

"So, are you up for a trip to the mainland tomorrow?" I asked Barb as I texted Julie to let her know we had the name of the restaurant where Carrie had lunch and the phone number of her date. We had a summary of a few other recent interactions, possibly a few leads.

She nodded, "Looks like The Captain's Deck opens at 11:00 a.m. So, what do you think? How about the 10:15 ferry?"

"Want to meet at Books & Brew? I'll get Buddy settled, do a little work, and set up for the Coin Collectors Club. They're having their meeting at the store tomorrow morning. I'll get a few things knocked out before we head over, and I will let you know how Julie responds to what I sent her. Maybe she will have an update for us too."

Julie answered my earlier text as I climbed into bed. She did have some updates and would meet me at Books & Brew first thing tomorrow. My mind replayed Carrie's texts as I settled beneath my light duvet. Her online personality seemed happy and maybe even a little flirty. As I drifted to sleep, I imagined tomorrow would be the day I might begin to understand the real Carrie.

Chapter 10

When Buddy and I arrived at Books & Brew, the sun had not yet painted the sky that special shade of Mongin Island Blush that promises a glorious sunny day. Everything was still and quiet, which gave me time to pull together a plan for the day. Turning on the lights and ceiling fans was a good start, but I also thought today was a day for peaceful background piano music. I bristled at remembering how the beach cottage felt yesterday and decided I wanted the store's vibe to balance that heaviness.

Julie arrived shortly after the first carafe of English breakfast tea was brewed. "Did you eat yet? I brought you a blueberry muffin."

Grabbing seats at the Trading Floor's farm table, I quickly logged into Carrie's computer while Julie fixed herself a mug of tea. We breezed through the text strings, and I updated her on the restaurant Barb and I were planning to visit in a few hours. We covered a lot of ground, even before our tea cooled to sipping temperature.

"Essentially, it seems Carrie met Charles at The Captain's Deck for lunch. We know she came back to the island alone. Captain Fred confirmed she was on the 3:45 boat on Monday, and she sat alone for the whole ride," Julie said as she brushed a few crumbs from her blue uniform pants. "Makes you wonder, right?"

She kept her gaze focused on the Mongin Island photos hanging on the wall behind me and continued, "We have been working with her phone and its location. I read the texts too, but you know, hearing you read them now—I have to say, they sound different, warmer, maybe ... what's the word? Maybe more hopeful. I'm glad you made visiting the restaurant a priority. It was on my list for tomorrow, it just didn't sound like there was much to this meeting, but I get a different vibe now hearing aloud what she could have said. The staff may be able to tell us how this meeting actually went, so I will follow up behind you. Funny thing, that is, to hear the words come alive like that."

"What do you think of my theory on Carrie's friends? It's weird, right? They had her computer, it's weird they didn't read her messages or share what they knew, don't you think?"

Julie brought her gaze to me. Her customary teal-lined eyes locked on my face. "Hold on, before we go there, I want to tell you we reached out to Charles Anders, Carrie's Monday date. His name wasn't in the contacts on her phone, but we got the info we needed from his phone number and his dating app profile. I left a voicemail, and Lieutenant Cole tracked him down to the River Street Hotel in Savannah."

She looked at her notebook, "And we also reached out to that other guy you mentioned, Thomas. According to him, they never met, and he is traveling out of state, so they definitely did not meet in the last few days. Lastly, seems Miss Carrie shut down her profile on the dating app. Well, maybe not closed it down, but she paused it. Took herself off the market, so to speak."

"That tells me Carrie felt something significant from her interactions, she felt some kind of connection. I hope you hear from Charles soon. I want to see if he can tell us more about Carrie, things her friends haven't or won't share," I said.

"Yes, things they won't share. To answer your question: I agree with you. Beginning with the way Carrie's absence was described through everything, including the computer, everything is on my radar ... but let's see where it takes us. First step is finding out what we are dealing with—we don't know this is a crime yet. The coroner's report should arrive before noon. You will likely still be on the mainland, but I will let you know what I hear."

After Julie left, I dove into readying the store for the day. The ordinary, routine tasks provided a structure that I always embraced. At the heart of it, I am a creature of habit. I was so absorbed in these tasks and thinking through Julie's visit that I didn't notice the guest sitting in the wood rocker closest to the front door. I swung the door almost right into his chair as I went to straighten up the porch.

"Good morning, sorry to keep you waiting! I didn't see you out here. Books & Brew won't open for some time. Can I get you a cup of tea while you wait? I am about ready to—"

My visitor popped up. His tan pants and tucked-in button-down shirt made me momentarily rack my brain for a vendor appointment I had perhaps forgotten about. He didn't look like a day tourist here to grab a paperback with which he could fill his afternoon. "I'm hoping you can help me, I'm not sure where else to go. The ferry crew directed me here," he cut me off.

Before I could ask, he blurted, "Do you happen to know Carrie Nichols? She is about my height, long blonde hair. She is visiting here, with her friends, and I need to connect with her. Yesterday certainly didn't go as planned, and now, I've lost my phone. I've tried calling her from my work phone, but she hasn't answered. Maybe it's just that she doesn't recognize my other number. I need to find her." He searched my face expectantly.

"Carrie? From Atlanta?" I tried to process the universe's unbelievable sense of timing. It was as if Julie and I had willed him into appearing here. "Are you Charles?"

"She mentioned me? I'm Charles Anders. It is nice to meet you!" I shook his offered hand, but I know I didn't hide my shock.

I held open the door, "Come inside, Charles. Please, come in, and let's have something to drink." I pointed him to the Trading Floor as I went to get us both mugs of tea. "Charles Anders is here with me at Books & Brew," I texted Julie before heading to the table.

"Charles, there is no easy way to say this …" I met his ice-blue eyes across the farm table and saw a flash of confusion and likely concern.

He was inadequately prepared for the words I was about to say. I paused and then started with, "I'm sorry to tell you that Carrie, well ..."

"What?" he demanded, "What about Carrie?"

"The thing of it is, Charles, we aren't sure yet what exactly happened. Unfortunately, Carrie has ... passed away. She left her cottage and somehow ended up on the beach, well into the dunes. When Carrie was found, she had already passed. I'm sorry for your loss."

Charles flash-froze in front of me. I don't recall him even blinking. "That's really not at all funny, I don't know what kind of humor you have but ... you can't be serious right now." He unfroze just as quickly and gathered himself and the few belongings he had previously emptied from his pockets.

"The ferry crew directed you to my store because I'm helping Deputy Julie and her team here on the island. The crew knew I would be able to give you the latest information. I know this is terribly shocking. Please, sit and let me help you." I pointed to the chair he had just abandoned.

Charles' athletic frame eventually crumpled into the ladderback chair, still angled away from the table, giving me his side profile. "Tell me what you know, tell me everything."

Sharing the details of the past days didn't take long, but he took his time hearing it all. Finally, he looked at me, straightened his chair, and cleared his throat. "You're missing quite a few things," he said, matter-of-factly. "Not much of an investigation, I've got to say."

I was, for once, at a loss for words. "Well then Charles, help me out. How about you tell me?"

"Carrie and I have been talking for weeks, you're right about that. And we did just meet for the first time in person at lunch on Monday. She was exactly as she sounded over text and on the phone, which is very rare. It was the first time in a long time that I didn't want a date to end." The reclaimed wood floor absorbed the beat of his hard leather-soled shoes as he paced around the room. It creaked in all its usual spots as he circled. I watched his long fingers weave their way through his sandy brown hair.

His words spilled out, "I had to break and get back to work. Carrie said there was someone else she was meeting near the restaurant and then she would head back to Mongin. We planned a breakfast picnic on the beach Tuesday. I had a few open hours in the morning, and she thought her friends wouldn't miss her too much."

"Did you ask her who she was meeting?"

"She didn't offer, and I didn't ask. Been a while since you've been in the dating scene? Hard to push someone you just met, right?"

Ouch. His reprimand stung. My ability to read people usually served me well. I had grown up being an observer of human behavior. But these circumstances were new to me; maybe I really didn't know how to navigate difficult conversations like these as I thought I did. "I didn't say push, I would think you would have wanted to know if she was seeing someone else." Fighting the urge to explain myself to him, I continued, "So, why didn't yesterday go as planned, as you said?" He put me on the defense. I'm not proud of that, but it was true.

He seemed unfazed or uninterested in his effect on me and he explained matter-of-factly. "We met at the gate to the public beach, as Carrie asked. She didn't tell me anything about her time on the island. I get that she didn't want me to come to her hotel room or wherever she was staying. I mean, we had just met and she was here with others, I didn't expect that. I brought the bagels, and fruit, as we said. She brought the beach blanket. We planned it all as we were walking down from the restaurant's top deck before we went our separate ways. Not that there was much to plan, but I was excited to know she wanted to see me again. It started fine enough, but it was not the same Carrie. Not the same Carrie at all."

Sighing, he continued, suddenly contrite, "Was it me? I don't know, that's why I wanted to talk to her. She was uncomfortable, didn't eat a single thing I brought, looked completely miserable. After I don't know, maybe ten long minutes of silence, fidgeting, and looking at anything else but me she asked if we could do it another day. Well, to be clear, she *asked* but really, she told me. That was the way it was going to be, just like that. No explanation, nothing. She stood up, put her sandals on, and walked away. Didn't take the blanket, didn't say goodbye. Just like that, she was gone."

"Was that the last you spoke to her? Did you follow her? Walk after her?"

"She asked me to leave her alone, so that's what I did." He answered with a finality that rocked me. Why did everyone in Carrie's circle seem so reluctant to contribute to the puzzle we were working to solve?

"I'm out of here," he said. "Nothing much for me to do. I had nothing to do with this, and I'm not getting involved in … whatever this is." He once again grabbed his keys, sunglasses, and pocket trinkets. "I wondered if this was too good to be true. If she liked me, then why was she meeting someone else? You said it yourself; she never should have done that. Nothing ever works the way it should. Not for me, anyway." His voice rose with each sentence, to the point where he was practically shouting as he lamented his lot in life.

His turbulent temper rattled me, from hopeful to almost hateful in a matter of minutes. Maybe Carrie sensed it, too, and had been hiding, just as Mary Frances said. As I watched Charles speed out of my parking lot, the sinking possibility of another Mongin murder was suddenly very real.

Chapter 11

"He's gone? I got here as fast as I could!"

"Just like that, gone," I said, snapping for emphasis. I summarized the highlights for Julie, ending with Charles' proclamation of innocence. "So, the breakfast date is now the starting point of this, I guess, right?"

"I will check with the ferry office to confirm he was a passenger for the trips he described," Julie said. "We will regroup after you and Barb go to the restaurant. I'm on my way to the medical examiner's office and then headquarters. Let's compare notes when you're done."

The ride to the ferry landing was not long enough to cover all the details, and we knew that the boat was not the place to finish our conversation. It would have to wait. "Well, this all took a turn quickly," Barb commented as we settled on the boat's bench seat, with our backs to the engines. We spent some of the ride catching up on the other events of the past few days.

"You met Poppy, have you met Dan?" she asked. "I heard he has been setting up on the beach and painting from a few different spots. Did you bump into him yet?"

"These days have been consumed with all this, but I am glad Dan has started on his project. It's like a movie, isn't it? A lone painter working quietly on an empty beach. That visual is its own art."

Barb chatted with some neighbors and left me to my thoughts, which was exactly what I needed. I watched the dolphins poke their heads above the water, keeping the boat in their sightline. How I loved this ride, this island, this community. This simple joy of being on the water, feeling the saltwater spray on a sunny day, calmed me in a way nothing else could. Before moving to Mongin full-time, I had no idea how much I needed this island and its people.

My life in Atlanta was full of all "the things", but it was missing the connection and community that are the roots of my life now. Most of the large city anonymity was lost on me in the busy days of raising children, building a career, and running a home. Our social calendar had been so filled that I missed the realization that I was empty. Running from thing to thing, with other people who were also living life at warp speed, often left us all distracted and drained. On Mongin, for better or worse, island life practically requires you to care about your neighbors. For it to work, we needed to know we could count on each other. In less than one year, I had been woven into the fabric here and I finally, truly, felt like a part of something.

Some days, the thirty-minute ferry ride passed in a blink. This was not one of those days. I was anxious to get to the mainland and find out more about Carrie's time with Charles. It had been years since I last ate at The Captain's Deck, and I was struggling to picture the sequence of events Charles described. The short walk from the ferry landing to the waterfront restaurant gave me a few minutes to finish updating Barb.

Deep in the details, relaying Charles' words and the way he shared them, I completely missed that Barb had stopped walking. It took me a few feet to realize she was no longer on my left. As I turned to find her, her face told me she felt the same way I did. There were too many oddball things for them all to be a coincidence.

"So, he is not interested in what happened to Carrie? Is that what he told you?" Disbelief and anger filled the distance between us as she quickly caught up to me. "Not a fan of this yin and yang in his temper either."

"Watching it unfold in front of me … it was very concerning. I'm likely not doing his reactions justice. Chilled me to the core. It wasn't a long conversation, but you know how it is with some people? The expectation, the emotion … it just seemed to last forever. He was unpredictable and I was waiting, watching his next move, not really sure where we were going next. With Carrie pausing her profile, she clearly was into him, but it makes you wonder, right? Did she see something when they were at lunch that made her not want to pursue this? Maybe she thought about it all overnight, and when she saw him, she knew she wanted to end things before they started."

Justin, the restaurant manager, was setting up the sidewalk signage listing the daily specials and offered to seat us as soon as we approached. "Hello and welcome! Table for two? It's a great day for the upper deck, or we have plenty of seating here at street level. What's your preference?" He straightened his name tag and wiped his hands on a black linen napkin tucked into his front pants pocket. His end-of-summer tan highlighted his bright smile and sun-freckled face.

It only took a minute to explain, and Justin showed us to a quiet table in the corner of the restaurant. "This time of year, lots of our staff head back to college. Things start to quiet down, so our management team doubles up on shifts. Me and Kendra, we're on the schedule every day for the next two weeks, so one of us would have been here. You know how it is, we're the host, the server, sometimes the bartender, and definitely a sous-chef. Tell me what you need, I'm sure we can help."

Showing him Carrie's picture and describing Charles got the ball rolling. "Wait a minute, was this Monday or Tuesday?" he asked immediately. "It was Monday, right?"

"Yes, Monday for lunch, right around noon," I said, sensing we were on to something.

"Monday wasn't that busy. Except for the summer months, when we are pretty slammed, Mondays are usually dead. I covered the upper deck, and I am pretty sure I remember these two. The lady wore a big straw hat, if I am thinking of the same person. The ribbon on the hat matched her blue shirt. She had one of those shirts where the sleeves have cut-outs for the shoulders … you know what I mean?"

Barb looked at me, "Those 'cold-shoulder' tops?" I nodded my agreement.

"Cold shoulder? Ha! She wasn't giving him any cold shoulder, that's for sure." Justin rolled his eyes, which hid behind a wave of brown hair that fell across his face. "She looked like she was having the time of her life, like this guy was a regular comedian. She was laughing and smiling. It didn't look like the first dates I usually see. This seemed like they both had a great time, really. They were both super friendly. It seemed I was interrupting every time I brought something to the table or checked on them."

"The lady was meeting someone else, after her lunch. Did you see her speak with anyone besides her date? Did you notice where she went or which way she headed as they left?" Now that their lunch was officially confirmed, I hoped we could find out more.

"I didn't notice, sorry. You know, we see some characters, especially during the busy season, but this looked like just a regular lunch, not really too much to it, at least not what I saw." Something caught his eye, and he slowly offered, "But maybe … I'm thinking about our security cameras—three in the front and two in the back of the restaurant. They pretty much give us a visual of our entire perimeter, plus a little extra. Sometimes we have some shenanigans, and it is good to have video. You're welcome to look at all the footage from Monday if you want." He pointed to the pillar across from us with a white camera aimed toward the street. "We keep the film for a week and then we record over it. You're in luck."

Although The Captain's Deck hadn't been busy Monday afternoon, foot traffic around the harbor's storefronts was decent. Crammed in the restaurant's back office, it took us some time to find Carrie and Charles on the footage. After a quick hug, Charles left Carrie near the street side tables. In a blink, he was gone, but Carrie remained, looking left and right.

"There goes our hero ..." Barb pointed to the screen. She was still mulling over Charles' earlier behavior.

"Too bad we can't see Carrie's face, with her back to us and that enormous hat. I'm assuming it's her, but who can tell? Would love to see if she looks happy, or if this is even her!"

"Wait, there she is, it's her!" Barb's excitement brought my eyes back to Justin's computer. It was Carrie. She took off her hat, shook out her hair, and waited. Using all of the different camera angles, we were able to see a petite woman in a long sundress soon approach Carrie. There was a light embrace but then an immediate distance. A few frames later, the two women walked away from The Captain's Deck and crossed the street.

Justin was just as excited as we were to see Carrie on screen, "Looks like they might be grabbing coffee at The Half Hitch." He brought up the feed from the camera focused on the front of the restaurant as well as the area directly across the street. We watched them enter a shop through a black door adorned only with a painted cream-colored knot.

Barb laughed, "It's like a speak-easy. I wouldn't have guessed that was a coffee shop! Seems if you know, you know." Based on the crowd coming and going, a lot of people did know. Like the ice cream shop a few doors down, this was a happening hot spot.

We soon saw Carrie emerge, alone, and head quickly towards the ferry dock. She was carrying her unfinished drink in a tall plastic cup. Her companion left the store a few minutes later, walking quickly, in the opposite direction, toward the parking lot. Their brief meeting was over.

Justin texted me the screenshot of the woman Carrie met and emailed me the digital files so I could share them with Julie. He encouraged us to ask for Tessa or Marly when we went to The Half Hitch, and we were soon on our way.

The shop was filled with delicious smells of coffee, sweets, vanilla, and cocoa. We met Marly as she filled our order. Her jet-black hair was piled on top of her head, and it matched the polish on her stubby fingernails. Carrie had made no impression on Marly, "Yeah, I was here Monday, been here all week, as usual. Can't place this face." She handed Carrie's photo back to Barb and asked nothing else.

We waited while she whipped up exotic brews with big puffy clouds of cream and squiggly designs stenciled into mugs full of coffee blends. Marly moved with an almost intentional indifference to us, to her customers, to everything it seemed.

Barb turned her back to the counter and said, "How many different ways are there to have a cup of coffee? Feels like we just heard every possible combination. This is taking forever ..." Barb said what I was thinking. When there was finally a brief break in the action, we jumped into the questions about Carrie's coffee companion. Handing Marly my phone so she could see the image from the security footage, I held my breath. Given the number of people moving through the store, I was not optimistic that the grainy image would mean much to Marly.

"Ahhh the vanilla bean, sweet cream cold brew lady, yeah, I know her. Well, I don't know her, but I know she is a regular. She comes in, like three, four, five days in a row at once, always carrying these enormous, bright leather tote bags. Sometimes she is here a few times a day, always ordering the same thing. Then we won't see her for a few weeks, but then she reappears. She pays through our app and leaves a cash tip in the jar every time. Same routine for months now. The name on her order is Galina, but in my mind, I call her Galina the Vanilla Beana. It's my way of remembering customer's names. You know, you make up some association, helps to lock it in here." She gently knocked her forehead and turned to rinse out the tools of her trade.

"Look on the bulletin board over there, she posted a supply of business cards on it. I know she does some resume work. It's a cool card, black with gold letters, matches our vibe here." She vaguely pointed the wood tamper she was holding toward the back of the store. Barb returned in a flash, triumphantly holding the card.

"Got it. Galina George, resume writer, right here." Barb tapped the card on her fingertips, "Phone number, email, and social media contacts. Let's go."

Chapter 12

Part of living on a bridgeless island was relinquishing the independence to get home when you wanted to. The next ferry was scheduled in thirty-five minutes, so we had time to fill. "Let's grab a seat and regroup, my head is spinning." Barb pointed to the bench facing the water, close to the dock.

"How about I touch base with Julie? She should have the medical examiner's report by now, and I also want to check in with Mary Frances, Annabelle, and Tracy. Maybe we can call Galina too before we get on the boat. But depending on the results in the report, we may never need to speak to Galina the Vanilla Beana." I concurrently outlined my plan and tried to lighten the mood.

As I waited for Julie to answer, Barb slowly shook her head, "I have a feeling we are going to be speaking with her soon. I just feel it."

Julie answered my call on the first ring, but I was not fully anticipating the entirety of her verbal download. Making eye contact with Barb, I motioned the universal signs of writing. She dug through her backpack and handed me her spiral notebook with her stick pen wedged in the side rings. I scribbled as Julie spoke. Barb tilted the pad, absorbing the words: rosary pea, vines, prolific, ingested, Florida/ Georgia/South Carolina, one seed, like ricin.

Carrie's family and friends had been told; everyone now knew—
Carrie had been poisoned.

"I called Carrie's mom. Man, that one was tough. The poor lady
is heartbroken. Fortunately, Carrie's sister was with her. And I just
left the cottage, which was a mixed bag. Kind of on brand for them,
crying, anger, and Tracy's usual silence. Annabelle, well, she had a
million questions, and we don't have all the answers, yet, obviously. I
asked them to stay another day or two. They are anxious to get back
to Carrie's mom but agreed to stay through Saturday. I'm not quite
ready to let them head off the island—if they will voluntarily stay, it
would be easier on us all. They agreed."

The implications of those words added weight to the situation. I
didn't ask and Julie didn't say, but Carrie's friends seemed to be "people of interest", at the minimum. After a call to Galina, we planned to
head back to Mongin and meet at Books & Brew later tonight.

"Galina?" Barb asked, handing me the black business card.

"I don't even know what to say to her, where to begin. What should
I ask her? I wasn't expecting Carrie to be poisoned. I thought maybe a
coronary issue or blood clot, or I don't know, some other catastrophic
medical event, not this ... poisoned by the seed of a plant that prolifically grows throughout the southeast?" In front of us, the water
sparkled its usual blue-green beauty, but I don't think either of us
focused on it. I was lost in understanding the idea that Carrie was
poisoned in plain sight.

I continued, "Honestly, I thought we were coming here today to
find out a few tidbits that could help Carrie's friends and family have
some closure. I thought we would be able to tell them that Carrie
was happy, beginning a new relationship, moving forward toward her
personal goals. I didn't think ... well, I didn't think we would be here,
again ..."

"Let's just take her temperature, see what kind of a vibe we get,"
Barb encouraged, "but put your volume up so I can hear, too." She
scooted closer to me. Galina's phone rang and rang, and then went
to voicemail. This left me equally relieved and deflated. I wanted

answers but didn't yet have all the questions. At the end of it, I didn't
have either.

After Books & Brew closed for the day, Tripp, Barb, Julie, and I
settled around the farm table in the Trading Floor eating the pizza
Tripp had picked up from the Eagle's Nest. The big triangle slices
with their gooey cheese and garlicky sauce had just about silenced us
as we each worked through a few pieces. Many napkins later, Julie was
ready to cover the details of our day. "It's time to dig in. Sheriff Oxley
thinks we need to beef up our presence on the island, you know, with
this being the second murder in a few months. Maybe twice-a-week
patrols are no longer enough."

She fired up her laptop, rolled up her sleeves, and asked us about
the video footage we emailed earlier. Before we could answer, Tripp
stood to start gathering the remnants of our meal, "If it's all the same
to you, I'm going to head out. Is there anything y'all need before I go?"

Julie spoke first, "I'm good, and thanks for dinner, Tripp. You
never know, we may need you … you were a big part of getting the
deal done in our last island case."

Sensing his discomfort with that possibility, I jumped in, "No, you
go ahead, Tripp, and thanks for dinner and for watching the store
today. I'll see you tomorrow."

"I'll help you if you need it, but I would rather not know all the
details right now. Knowing Carrie was poisoned, here on Mongin …
I'm going to need some time to let that sink in. I can't just pretend
these things don't matter or don't change things—they do. This is not
the Mongin I know, the Mongin I came here for. I'm not sure how I
feel about this." He started toward the little kitchenette, on the other
side of the store. Before he was out of the room, I heard him say quietly, probably more to himself than to us, "Maybe this isn't my place
after all." Mongin was the refuge he sought after his own heartbreak
of losing his wife and daughter. I understood his need to be on solid
ground after his world had shattered.

"When he is ready, *if* he is ready, he will let us know," I said. "Until
then, Tripp decides what he wants to do with this case. This island,
this community needs him—we can't lose him. We have to help him

preserve the Mongin Island he wants and needs. Tripp will help us if he can when his time feels right—when he has thought through it. He can't be—he shouldn't be rushed." Carrying the weight of Tripp's worry, and the magnitude of all we had learned today shortened my fuse.

"I'm sorry, that was insensitive," Julie said quickly, looking at both of us as if I had scolded her—which was not my intention. She needed to know this was not just a job for us. We were here living among the worry, the uncertainty, and the suspicion. Of course this affected us. She continued, "He was such a help with getting to a confession last time, he was a natural. I was trying to include him, encourage him, not chase him away."

"Forgive us, Julie, we are amateurs at this sleuthing. You know how much Mongin Island means to us. It is the glue that holds us together. Many of us left our mainland cares behind when we packed up our stuff and barged it over here. It's hard for us to compartmentalize. This is our home, a home we love," I said, purposefully letting the words fill the space more gently and slowly. Still, after a year of living here, I hadn't mastered the art of the "non-direct/direct conversations" that happened all around me. In my past profession as a consultant, I was paid for my opinions. This wasn't a fact-filled project at the firm, this was a misunderstanding and me trying to protect someone who was perfectly capable of handling himself but was currently not able to decide how to move forward. I still had so much to unlearn.

Barb stepped in, as she sometimes does in her authentic way of bridging gaps, reminding us of the things we share, "I bet you a dozen donuts Tripp will tell us, in a day or two, that he is onboard and will be by our side trying to crack this case. Wait, I'll bet you one of Miss Lucy's pies. If I am wrong, I will spring for your favorite. Who's in? You know, Miss Lucy often will bake something based on a neighbor's need. This time, it might be one of you!"

We debated the prizes Barb may have to buy if we won the bet. I threw my hat in the ring for a chance at Miss Lucy's Banana Icebox pie. Her toasted graham cracker crust sealed the deal for me. A few days ago, Hetty, the owner of the general store where Miss Lucy sells her pies, mentioned this one was a possibility for the weekly pie delivery next Tuesday. This back-and-forth banter filled me with gratitude. We are people who want to do the right thing, care for each other, support each other, guide each other, and take on questions, concerns, and problems of all kinds. From solving crimes to debating pies, we tackled the problems head-on.

With her attention back on her laptop screen, Julie began again. "So, as far as we know, Charles may have been the last person to see her alive, but that does not necessarily mean he poisoned her at their failed breakfast date. Depending on the amount ingested, it can take anywhere from one to three days for a dose to be fatal." She paused and looked for her paper notes, which had not yet been entered into the case file.

Flipping the page, she continued, "Right, we have some testing that needs to come back. So far, we have the basic blood and urine analysis which, along with some other benchmarks, indicate a TOD of 7:00 to 9:00 p.m. Tuesday."

"Todd? Another dating app guy? Who is Todd?" Barb asked immediately, "How many people are we tracking right now?"

"Time of death," Julie and I answered together.

Barb laughed, "To your point, some of us are more amateur than others."

Julie continued, "Preliminarily, it appears Carrie ingested the poison twenty-four to thirty-six hours before her death—however, keep in mind, a single crushed seed, basically something that started smaller than a grain of rice, can be lethal. For now, it looks like she received 'a mediumly significant amount'. The report goes on to state the estimated metric weight of the dose, but does .002 mg mean anything to you?"

We both shook our heads, and Julie went on. "Cytology will be back tomorrow before noon and will help us narrow down the ingestion window. For now, we can assume, she was poisoned while on vacation—either at her cottage, the chili cook-off, her lunch date, or some other place she visited, and we have yet to know."

"Don't forget the coffee with Galina," Barb reminded.

Julie nodded, "Right, that's all part of the lunch date timeframe. And there is something else, something that is definitely curious. We got access to Carrie's bank records and other personal information, as you would expect. It is all pretty straightforward stuff. She had a few credit cards, car payments, and a mortgage on her condo, all standard. Her salary is deposited directly, again not surprising. One thing we are exploring is that she had a separate savings account with an online bank. It was opened about five years ago, with monthly deposits of $5,000. The money was always wired in from a foreign account. No withdrawals, no transfers, just a bunch of money sitting there."

Julie looked at us, "That's a lot of money for someone at Carrie's income level. Looks like a settlement, or some kind of structured payment. We can't find any indication she was a party to legal action that would have resulted in a payout."

"A foreign account? What ties does Carrie have to foreign entities? No one has mentioned anything like that." I started to question how we would tackle this.

Julie raised her hand, "We are on this, we are looking into finding out more about all this."

"Until we know otherwise, I think we should focus on knowing more about Galina, Charles, and I hate to say this, but Carrie's friends, too. To your point, Julie, maybe there was someone else she met or another place she visited. But those people, places, and potential motives are unknown to us, for now," I said.

"Keep in mind, random crimes where the victim and the suspect are strangers ... well, they are actually pretty rare. Almost 80% of homicide victims are known or related to their killer. But with intentional poisoning, which is already such a small percentage of total homicides, that number is almost 100%. These are statistics, of course, not definites. I just want to make sure you understand the potential for Carrie to have ingested rosary pea, given to her by a stranger, is statistically almost nonexistent."

The idea that Carrie's friends or even Charles had harmed her made her death even sadder. These were all people she trusted, to varying degrees. "I can start to learn more about Charles and Galina, dig into their relationships, stuff like that," I offered.

Julie stood. "Thank you, both. This is a great start. We are managing the cellular data, the location services, and all this background information like the finances. I am also reaching out to Carrie's family. I want to hear their perspective on Carrie's last days. I will also give you an update on the medical and forensic information as it comes in. That may help firm up the timeline, the sequence of events."

She zipped her laptop into its case and continued, "Today has been a full day, and I'm thinking tomorrow will be as well. Between all the science and then the conversations you plan to have, let's regroup mid-day and see where things land. Do you think if Tripp knows this was likely not a random act of violence, it may help him?"

Julie's compassion made her an excellent police officer, and friend. "I think so, don't you agree, Barb?" I smiled at them both.

"When he is ready and you two are buying my pie, I think we will all feel better," she agreed as we closed and locked the door behind us.

Chapter 13

Sleep was nowhere to be found. Tossing and turning most of the night, I finally gave up well before my alarm chimed. My mind was anxious to start processing everything I learned in the last few days. All the information, conversations, facts, and figures were scattered like the different kinds of shells on the Rosemont Inn beach. Buddy and I ate our breakfasts and we headed there for a long walk. I needed to get organized.

The sun was already out, and it would be a practically still-summer warm day soon enough. For right now, the hint of chill helped us with our brisk walk. In these moments, this beach belonged only to us. Buddy had been cooped up in the store for the last few days. He was ready to run along the sand a few feet from the water and dig with his two front paws working in unison. I tossed a few sticks to him, which he dutifully chased but did not retrieve. He returned to me, over and over, with his tail wagging in a circle, showing me his pure joy at spending time together while concurrently forgetting he had retriever DNA. This dog was one of the best things that happened to me since moving here.

"Buddy, let's head home and get ready for our day. Ready, good boy?" He dutifully gave his black coat a prolonged shake and fell in step next to me. It was strange to be back on the beach where Carrie had been found. The neon yellow crime scene tape was gone, there was no physical indication of all that had happened here, but nothing felt normal. I made a silent promise to Carrie that we would do our best to solve this case for her and all of Mongin Island.

Setting up Books & Brew for the day included unpacking a few boxes of new arrivals and selections for my local author shelf. My mind was occupied, which helped my body work. Floors were swept, tea was brewed, pillows were fluffed, and counters and shelves were wiped down. The store was ready for customers before the first golf cart rattled down Old Port Passage Way.

It was still early, but the anticipation of learning more got the better of me and I dialed the number Charles had provided.

"Charles Anders," he answered on the second ring, almost like he had been waiting for my call.

"Charles, hi, it's Carr Jepson, from Mongin," I paused, waiting for some acknowledgement, recognition, or a social clue of any kind. Receiving none, I continued, "I have some updates for you. Hoping you had a few minutes, there are several things I want to talk to you about. Does now work for you?"

He sighed, "What? What do you want to ask me?"

Interesting … He defensively wanted to know how he was going to be involved, more than anything I was going to share about Carrie … very interesting.

"We know what happened to Carrie," I paused again, processing his reaction, absorbing what he said, what he didn't say. "I am sorry to tell you, well, it seems Carrie was poisoned."

It seemed at least a few minutes passed before he said, "Poisoned? What is that supposed to mean?"

I didn't know how I could have been any clearer. "It means—"

He cut me off, "You are saying someone gave her some kind of poison? This was done *to* her? Not like her eating or drinking or touching something accidentally?"

"Yes, we believe that to be true. We believe this to be intentional, given the amount and specific type of poison. This is not something that would have been problematic if she touched it. It is only poisonous if she ingested it. Based on the preliminary medical reports, she ingested it after her arrival to Mongin. It's relatively fast-acting, unlike other poisons, I've since learned." The longer it went without him saying anything to stop me, the more my words kept coming and coming. I forced myself to quit babbling.

We sat with this information between us, a rock each of us was waiting for the other to push. After a few more minutes, he cleared his throat and said, "And, so what did you want to talk to me about? I've told you everything I know about her, what more do you want from me?"

"I want to understand more about your two in-person meetings. Tell me about your lunch date, even the details that you don't think matter, things like what you ate and drank, what you talked about, where you sat. You know, stuff like that. Tell me if Carrie checked her phone while you were eating. Did she leave the table during your meal? Did she talk to anyone else at the restaurant? I also would like to know more about the few minutes before and after Carrie decided your breakfast date was over. Did you see where she walked to, how she got there? Thank you, for anything you can share."

Most of these details Justin had already given us, but I was curious to hear if Charles would speak truthfully. He seemed very put out by it all, but even so, he complied. He ran through a summary of their time together, ticking items off a list, without any unnecessary words and almost no emotion. For the most part, Charles' answers mirrored what we already knew, nothing raised a flag until he said, "The only time she touched her phone was when we first sat down at the table on the upper deck. She texted someone and then moved her phone into her bag. But since you already saw her messages, and have her phone, you know more about that than I do. I assume she was texting her friends to tell them I wasn't a creep or to tell them she had arrived safely, or something like that. It was just a quick thing; I didn't really think much about it."

He spoke of something that didn't exist. There were only two texts on Carrie's phone that morning. One was to her mother, with some details about her trip and vague information about the day Carrie planned. The other text was to Charles saying she was on the boat, on her way. Why would Carrie pretend to text someone? Was she fearful of him, letting him think that others knew of her location? If so, then why didn't she tell anyone where she was?

Because I had read her messages, as Charles said, I wasn't asking him if Carrie texted anyone. He had heard a question that I hadn't asked. Instead, what I wanted to know was if she was checking her phone to see if there were incoming messages, maybe revealing some level of anxiety or concern about the meeting she was having after their lunch date. But this was an interesting twist, a curiosity Charles inadvertently provided.

He continued with details of Tuesday's beach breakfast. "The whole thing probably lasted thirty minutes. Took me longer to get there than the time we spent together, and in all transparency that made me mad. She certainly acted like so many girls before her, hot and cold. Everything was great the day before, and then she could barely even look at me the next day. I've been down this road many times. After a few minutes, she stood up and headed down the beach, away from the hotel. Like I told you, I didn't know where she was staying. It was all so weird."

"I know you also said you only had limited time, you had to work on Tuesday, right?" I encouraged him.

He said quietly, "I'm not proud of it, but yes, I was mad, very mad, and I guess you could say embarrassed. I walked quickly to the beach parking lot. I saw a man and a woman heading toward the beach from one of the houses near the walkway. Gave them the shopping bag of food, got in my cart, and made it to the ferry. Lucky for me, I only had to wait ten, maybe fifteen minutes till they were boarding the next boat. Not much to report. You know, after I cooled down, I tried to reach Carrie and then, well, the rest is history. I saw you and you told me all that happened, that's all I know."

"Thank you, Charles, this is exactly the information I needed, it's super helpful. Just a few more things. The ferry company has confirmed your itinerary. Do you happen to remember anything about the people you saw near the beach? Or anyone else you may have spoken to? I'm not sure it will be helpful for Julie, but I would like to give her everything we know."

He answered quickly, "I can't remember what they looked like, nothing too special about them. The lady was small, the man had gray hair. The only thing I can tell you is that he was carrying an easel and a small wooden chair. She had a canvas tote that looked almost like a toolbox. I think it was filled with tubes of paints and brushes. It all happened quickly, I handed the lady the bag and kept walking. I don't remember saying much of anything to her. Probably won't be too hard to find people who set up on the beach to paint."

He was right about that. I knew exactly whom I would visit next.

Chapter 14

Tripp hadn't arrived yet, but I felt I couldn't wait another minute. He likely would be at the store soon so I texted him, locked up, and was on my way.

He answered as I was backing up my cart, "Got a late start, but will be on my way in twenty minutes or so." It was very unlike Tripp to be delayed, and him "getting a late start" was something that had not happened once in the more than six months we had been working together. Something was off, and whatever it was, I wanted to get to the bottom of it as soon as I got back to the store.

My ride to the resort only took a few minutes and I was quickly in front of the large house right next door to the Inn. I pulled into the crushed stone driveway immediately after Poppy. She was balancing a cardboard takeaway box from the Dirt Road Diner, the food truck only minutes from Books & Brew. She smiled broadly as she grabbed a coffee from the cup holder. "You've been on my mind! So great to see you, Carr. Come in, we are feeling lazy today and decided to treat ourselves to these superb breakfast croissants. Want to split one with me?"

I followed her into her rental home. With its huge windows, light poured in from every direction, making the house feel endlessly spacious. "Thank you, Poppy. I'm so sorry to stop in without calling first and now, to interrupt your breakfast. Would you prefer for me to come back?"

"Nonsense! Sit down, and at least nibble on these berries I picked up at the farmers market on Old Port Passage. Hold on, let me get Dan before the food gets cold."

While she was gone, I took a seat at the table she had pointed to, which was built into a nook by the bay window. This magnificent view of the ocean was priceless, watching boats in the distance, listening to the waves, smelling the salt air. There was something for all the senses, making it clear why this house was their favorite.

"So, the Mongin Island celebrity, Carr Jepson, here in our midst!" A booming voice announced Dan's presence. He burst into the room, full of energy, shaking my hand, plating food, and moving around Poppy in some kind of unplanned choreography. My eyes followed him as I tried to answer the questions he fired off. I could tell immediately he was a man of endless curiosity. He wanted to know about my background, my island home, my family, and of course, Books & Brew.

Eventually, he pulled out a heavy oak chair across from me at the round pedestal table and unfolded the white paper napkin next to him by waving it to his side, wordlessly announcing the beginning of his meal. Poppy placed a steamy cup of coffee in front of me and that seemed to be Dan's cue to let her take the lead.

"So, Carr, I know we are going to get together soon, but tell me what this pleasant surprise is about. It is wonderful that Dan got to meet you today. We have been trying to get to the store, but he has been so productive, we haven't done too much island exploring yet."

I smiled at Dan, who was still busy with his breakfast, "I apologize for barging in, for not calling. I am helping Deputy Julie with her most recent case, and I learned something today that I wanted to ask you about. I got a little excited, a little ahead of myself."

"Not at all, this worked perfectly," Dan answered without making eye contact. "But who is Deputy Julie, and what case are you helping her with?"

I was so immersed in it all, it was unimaginable to me that someone would not already know the answers to Dan's questions. Dan and Poppy got the highlights, a summary of the past few days, how I got involved, and what we learned so far.

"Fascinating. So you are an entrepreneur, a former partner in a consulting firm, and a mother to two adult children. Now you are telling us you are also an amateur sleuth who partners with law enforcement because of your love of Mongin Island and your vast professional abilities. No wonder you're the talk of the town! This is very interesting, I have a lot of questions I would like to ask you, actually, starting with—"

"Dan, honey please, let Carr talk, she came here for our help." Poppy gently brought us back to the topic at hand.

"Dan, you're very kind, and I promise, when we get together in the next week or two, I will answer all your questions. Poppy is right, we are all working on different parts of the case. I've been spending time with some of the people who saw Carrie in her last few days. One of them is a man she met online a few weeks ago and then in person on the mainland on Monday."

We talked about Charles and arrived quickly at the breakfast date on Tuesday. "So based on Charles' description, it sounds to me like you may have been the recipient of their picnic wares as Charles headed to his cart. Do you remember that?" The question sounded ridiculous as soon as I said it. It's not like you're handed a bag of food by a stranger every day.

Poppy answered, "Yes, we were on our way to the beach, and we passed a young man who handed us the bag. He said, 'Here, take this, she didn't want it and neither do I' and kept walking. We had no idea what was going on. The whole thing was weird, so weird, right Dan?"

"Weird for those few minutes but then we got to the beach, well, then we knew."

"Knew what? What did you see? Did you see this woman, Carrie?" After I took out one of Carrie's pictures, I tightly wrapped my hands around the seat of the chair, trying to stay still.

"Figured there must have been a few of them, but only saw the man and the back of someone walking down the beach, heading toward the county dock. Looked like a lady, could have been this Carrie, I guess. But well, based on what they left behind, we thought they had just been out there partying, drinking, and hanging out there through the night, which is what got them in the shape they were."

"Dan, I'm not following this. What did you see? Tell me specifically."

Poppy answered for him, "It looked like someone had been sick on the beach. We assumed they had been there drinking. There were lots of places where someone had been sick. That's what he is trying to say. We didn't see any bottles or cans, so then we thought maybe it was some ill animal. We didn't know what to think. We moved further down the beach, away from it, in the opposite direction. Didn't really think too much more about it or the mystery man with his bag, I guess this Charles you mention. We threw his bag right into the trash can at the entrance to the beach, at the top of the dunes, and haven't given it any more thought."

No wonder Carrie didn't want to sit with Charles on their breakfast date. The poison was affecting her and making her sick. The tide had carried all that evidence away before we started searching for Carrie on Tuesday late afternoon. Now, hearing this, the pieces were beginning to click into place, firming up the timeline of events.

"Did you see Carrie again? After she walked away, did you see her again? Maybe later?" I asked.

Poppy and Dan exchanged a long look and then Dan answered, "Well, we didn't see her that day, no."

"But you did see her? Was it on another day?" I prompted.

"The windows, these amazing windows, and this glorious weather, yes, we saw her," he answered cryptically.

"Dan, you're frustrating me," Poppy said. "And I know what you're trying to say. I'm sorry, Carr. When he is in the artistic zone, it's a little like this. Creative with his vision, his thoughts, and his words. Can drive you crazy if you aren't expecting it. Yes, I think we saw Carrie a few times. Of course, we didn't know it was Carrie. I think we saw this woman and another woman, about her age, but shorter, walking together on the beach. It was all very animated and since our windows were open, and their voices carried, we could tell there was some heat, something that didn't sit well, between them. They both seemed angry, you could just tell from the body language. We only heard raised voices, we were too far away to hear their words. We saw them walking on Sunday and on Monday, and both times, things seemed tense."

After describing all three of Carrie's companions, I learned it was probably Tracy who was taking beach walks with Carrie.

A few minutes later, I was on my way back to Books & Brew. It had been a very productive hour. I knew I was going to need to spend a few minutes jotting down all the things I learned from Poppy and Dan, and I was starting to mentally sort them all as I pulled into the store's parking lot. I was relieved to see Tripp's cart in its usual spot, parallel to the front porch across from the front door. There were only two other carts in the lot, which meant I hopefully would have a few minutes with Tripp when these customers went on their way.

Tripp was behind the counter, busy helping the group, so I waited somewhat impatiently by the register. Tripp invited them to grab a cup of tea and enjoy the porch, which they seemed eager to do. We both seized the opportunity to clear the air the minute the front door shut behind them. Finally, I charged forward, in my usual "needing to know" tone.

"Tripp, I'm worried about you. You've been on my mind since last night and it just—" I started.

He started just a split second after me, "I have something I need to tell you." We looked at each other and the weight of that phrase halted my words.

"You first," I said, quieter, far less confident than I had been just a minute ago. I moved to the club chairs in front of the register and sat on the edge of the cushion. Tripp remained at the counter, his hands locked onto its rounded edge.

"Julie's words," he began and stopped. I wasn't sure if he could hear my heart pounding as I braced for him to tell me that he didn't sign up for being part of a 'detective agency', that he doesn't want to live

with uncertainty and the influx of crime and mystery. I was not ready
for another loss, but I tried to prepare to hear whatever he needed to
say.

"Julie's words should not have affected me like that. She didn't say
anything except that she wanted me to be included. I couldn't sleep
last night, hearing you come to my defense, trying to protect me. It
made me think long and hard, I tell you. At the heart of it, I've been
trapped in this post-grief world of losing my wife and my daughter,
not allowing myself to move forward. Frankly, I'm kind of sick of it
all myself. I'm sorry I have been like this, a burden in some ways, just
frozen from moving forward. I take one step forward and five steps
back."

What did he mean? My mind was racing to a conclusion, a guess
of what he was going to say next. I fought the urge to prompt him,
knowing this was his story, his terms that he was going to set. I
remained still and silent.

He went on, "I'm turning over a new leaf. I want to tell you that, I
am going to work very hard to do what Eloise and Michelle would
have wanted, to continue to live. You and Barb, you mean the world
to me. I am here to be part of the community, this specific community,
the way it is right now and will be going forward. I said it before and
now, I mean it. I can't hide, I won't hide anymore. Consider me part of
the team, whatever adventures we have, I want to be part of it all. The
parts I like, the parts I don't like. Consider me part of the detective
squad too, after Barb, of course."

Relief flooded me, grateful to have Tripp committed to staying on
the island. Tears stung the corners of my eyes. Yes, of course, I was
happy to have his help and insight for our work on Julie's cases. But
more importantly, most importantly, our friend would be remaining
here with us.

"Tripp, the idea of you leaving, for you to not feel at home on
Mongin, I couldn't bear it."

He smiled broadly and his eyes sparkled with excitement. "Well,
I'm not sure Barb should have any worry of me replacing her as your
official sidekick, but I think I made some decent progress very early

this morning." Our familiar Tripp was back with his gentle ribbing and kind sense of humor. I could tell he had something more to say, so I waited.

"Are you ready for this?" He paused and looked directly at me. Without waiting for my reply, he said, "It seems Charles Anders has had an interesting past. Just about five years ago, he was named as a person of interest in the death of Jessica Connors, his former girlfriend."

He handed me a package of printed online articles. A grainy picture of a younger Charles was in the top right corner of the cover page.

"That's the right Charles Anders, isn't it?" Tripp asked as he tapped the papers lying between us.

Chapter 15

"Call Julie, or text her, she needs to know," I said, feeling a seismic shift in the direction I had been mentally heading. "Have to say, I wasn't expecting this twist. Wow, Tripp, coming in hot with your contribution. You might replace both me and Barb, at this rate." I smiled at him, conflicted by the facts he revealed and my relief at knowing we weren't losing him.

"A person heads to her day job and gets replaced, just like that?" Barb greeted us with a laugh as she breezed into the store. "Clearly, I missed something, what's been going on this morning? You two look like you've seen a ghost." She settled in next to Buddy's chair and tossed him part of a dog cookie she pulled from her front pocket. Barb always had a treat ready for any pup she encountered in her travels.

I heard Tripp speaking with Julie, so I filled Barb in, working backward from the information regarding Charles to the exchange with Poppy and Dan. She was an active listener, nodding her head, raising her eyebrows, and gasping with the shock of the revelation regarding Charles. Her eyes were wide, and she sat processing all the information I just shared.

"Julie will be here in thirty minutes or so, she was boarding the sheriff's boat when I called. Said she would get the team updated on Charles and ask them to prioritize exploring his past. She has the medical reports and some information for us, too. Barb, you okay? You look like our ghost just visited you too!" Tripp took in the scene of us sitting together but miles apart in our thoughts.

"Let's move to the Trading Floor," I suggested and went to brew some fresh tea. I pulled out a big box of pimento cheese straws from my emergency stash hidden deep in the kitchenette's upper cabinet. We were going to need some provisions for this discussion.

A few customers came and went. Tripp and I took turns answering questions and ringing up a few small sales. In between, Barb got us organized by updating our case notes so we would be ready for this meeting with Julie. Lieutenant Cole and Julie arrived in no time, and we were all ready to dive in.

"Let's start with the forensic information," Julie said. "Here is a copy of the medical examiner's report. The first two pages are the director's summary. Simply said, abrin, which is found inside rosary pea seeds, is a powerful poison and lethal in small doses. Essentially, it shuts down the protein production in cells and causes a host of issues, including organ failure. Based on the RNA cytology analysis, Carrie ingested a little over four micrograms. Picture this dose looking like two sugar packets in size, roughly."

She looked up from her notes, "A good question might be, how did she ingest abrin without knowing? If Carrie had only been given the seeds found inside each pea and swallowed them without chewing, she likely would have been just fine. Abrin is only released when the seed's outer shell is broken. Grinding up the seeds, chewing them, those kinds of things make the poison accessible when consumed. This was a deliberate act, make no mistake about it. The ingestion timing has been narrowed to Monday between 12:00 and 5:00 p.m. Carrie's time of death is somewhere in the 12-hour range between Tuesday at 3:00 p.m. and Wednesday at 3:00 a.m."

"Poor Carrie, alone, outside, sick, organs failing," Barb said quietly, "What a horrific death."

"Delusion is also a symptom of abrin poisoning. Carrie may not have had the ability to find her way back to the cottage to get help. She may not have been well enough, physically or mentally. You're right, Barb, a very tough death," Lieutenant Cole agreed.

He continued, "This narrows down our primary suspects to people with access to Carrie—her friends in the cottage, Charles, and this mysterious coffee person, this ... Galina George. We have the means, conceptually. Now we need to understand possible motives and then, of course, opportunity. Who had the opportunity to access rosary pea and then, ultimately, access something Carrie was going to eat or drink?"

The cell phone location reports revealed nothing that came as a surprise. Carrie had been to the mainland, to various places on Mongin, all things we knew and expected. There were no hidden messages, text strings, or other funny business. I was happy to hear that, but before we moved on, I wanted to ask about Galina. "Just a question on the cell phone, was there any communication from Galina to Carrie? How did they know to meet on Monday afternoon? I didn't read any messages from her."

"Nothing at all, but we are looking at her landline. Believe it or not, she still had one of those back in Atlanta and we are pulling that activity now," Cole said quickly.

"I will ask Galina when I reach back out to her later today," I added. Julie and Cole nodded simultaneously.

"On the topic of Charles: wow, Tripp you stumbled onto some late breaking news. Kudos to you!" Julie said while Cole pulled up some additional notes on his laptop. "I want to let you know that at this moment, from what we can tell, Charles was never named as an official suspect in the death of Jessica Connors. Several officers on my team are researching the records, and contacting law enforcement in Georgia, right now. This may explain his actions over the last few days. Can't go through something like that and not have any baggage, that's for sure."

"This may make me sound cold and callous," I said, "but he still had the opportunity to hurt Carrie. He was with her around the ingestion window. Charles may well be very unlucky in love, but until we know otherwise, we are still keeping him on the suspect list, right? I mean, you have to admit, these are very strange coincidences."

"You're exactly right Carr, yes, he is on the person of interest list, along with Galina and all three of her travel companions. By the end of today, I would like to start narrowing it down so we can focus our efforts better."

With that goal in mind, we spent the next thirty minutes planning and assigning tasks.

Julie stood. "One last thing. Annabelle, Tracy, and Mary Frances are planning on leaving tomorrow. Let's make sure we think of anything else we need from them before they clear out—especially Tracy. I'm heading over there to check on them, but I think it may be a good idea to follow up with them after you speak with Galina. Carr, sorry to ask, but can you add this to your list for today, too?"

I nodded. "Yes, I was wondering if they knew anything about Galina, and if so, would they be willing to share it with us? How about we all regroup later today? Julie, Cole, are you planning to come back to the island?"

"How about a video call? We still have quite a bit to do with understanding more about Carrie, and some of her finances, background, relationships, and so on. We may not get back here today," Julie said as Cole packed up his laptop and notes.

After Julie and Cole headed out, the room was quiet as we digested the totality of this information and developed our own theories to explore. Finally, Tripp broke the silence, "After you reach out to Galina, then you're going to the cottage. How about I hold down things here and in between customers, want me to see what else I can learn about Galina George? It's been slow today, I probably will be able to have some time to work on this, if things stay as they are."

"I have to pop over to my rental down by the general store," Barb said. "They are checking out tomorrow and I want to review a few end of visit things with them. It should only take me about thirty minutes roundtrip. Carr, I can then come with you to the girls' trip beach cottage and run through the check-out instructions with them, too. Will that work?"

I answered them both, "Thanks, Tripp. Any information you can find on Galina would be great. She is definitely a mystery to us all at this point. I haven't been able to find too much yet." I looked at my watch and said, "Barb, want to swing back here when you're done with your visitors? We can head over to the beach cottage together when you're ready."

Barb scooted out the front door, armed with an agenda for the day. Tripp stationed himself at the register. Before heading to my office, Buddy and I took a quick walk outside. After a few minutes, I sat on the second porch step while Buddy leaned against my leg. We both seemed lost in our thoughts. He was likely watching the fox squirrels hop across the parking lot and lawn, but I was thinking about how to approach Galina, identifying the key things I wanted and needed to know. It was hard to separate how heavy this phone call felt, how much I wanted it to be fruitful from the possibility that this woman could be nothing more than Carrie's circumstantial, inconsequential meeting.

After all this introspection, I looked at Buddy, still leaning softly against my legs, as Labrador retrievers are known to do, and said, "Buddy, you've got the right idea. I need to just stay in the moment, not think about what could be, or what may be. Right?" His tail thumped a few times, and I took that as a sign I was on the right track. With this encouragement, I reached into my back pocket for my phone, scrolled through the history, and hit Galina's number.

Chapter 16

Being in the right frame of mind did nothing to put Galina on the other end of the phone. Once again, the call went to voicemail. This time my message was followed by an email and a social media inquiry. This felt like a defeat, and it sapped my energy.

"That was fast—how did it go?" Tripp asked as Buddy and I re-entered the store.

"It didn't, unfortunately. I'm really disappointed, we need to talk to her. Did you find anything?"

"Just some information about her resume writing business, social media info, stuff like that. It almost seems like she is not a real person. She shouldn't be this hard to find, right?"

I didn't immediately answer Tripp and after a few minutes, he looked up from his screen. "What? What are you thinking?"

"I'm thinking you may be on to something, Tripp. I just assumed this person was named Galina. I mean, she is a real person. We saw her on the security footage and Marly, in the coffee shop, recalled her immediately. But what if this is an alias? Then I have to wonder what she is hiding from."

"She could literally be anyone, I guess. I'm just thinking ... how will we ever figure this out?"

"Figure what out?" Barb asked from the doorframe. "What did I miss this time?"

"No luck with Galina, we aren't any further along. She didn't answer her phone, again, and neither of us learned anything more about her. Right, Tripp?"

"It's like she is a ghost." Tripped floated his arms above his head.

"So, who is she?" Barb asked rhetorically, then very seriously added, "Time for Operation Stakeout, I think."

Tripp and I were both not clear exactly what Operation Stakeout was. Based on the conviction with which Barb said it, it felt like a real thing, something we should know or would soon know.

"The what now?" Tripp asked, "I know I just joined this so-called detective agency or program or whatever it is you two do, but I think I missed the training on Operation Stakeout. What's the plan?"

Barb's eyes went from Tripp to me, then back again. I found myself leaning into the space between us, waiting for my marching orders. Instead, Barb threw her head back and laughed. "You two, you're cut from the same cloth. So literal!" Gathering herself, she continued, "How about we take the next boat over to the mainland and see if Galina needs a Vanilla Beana? Hopefully, we can meet her in person at the coffee shop. What else can we do? I am open to any and all suggestions."

"Who knows if she is still in the area? Remember Marly said she comes for a few days, then disappears for a few weeks. But I guess it's worth a try. We don't have anything to lose, that's for sure. Tripp, you good with the store?"

He nodded, "I'm good, and I'm happy the only stakeout I'm going on is one within the walls of this place!"

"I'll drive us to the ferry landing. Barb, please text Julie to let her know about the change of plans. How about we swing by the cottage on the way back? Maybe we can bring Tracy, Annabelle, and Mary Frances some dinner. I haven't seen them at all, not once around the resort, at the Beach Club, not even walking around. Maybe dinner will give them a little break."

Barb nodded, "I'll text them, too. Maybe we can pick up a sandwich tray at that cute cafe a few doors down from the coffee shop. They had their menu posted in the window."

"I was actually thinking of getting takeout from The Captain's Deck, maybe touching base with Justin or the other manager, Kendra. What do you think?"

"The cafe will have to wait, your idea is better! Tripp, what do you want for dinner? We'll bring you back something, too. Text me when you decide, we will grab it." We also decided we would meet at my house later today. Tripp would close the store and bring Buddy home.

"I feel like we have spent the last few days making plans and assigning tasks, lots of 'to-dos' but nothing to really show for it. Do you feel like we're spinning our wheels a little?" I asked Barb as we climbed into my cart.

"I agree it has been a little harder to get momentum going, probably because of the stages we have walked through, right? First, Carrie was missing, then we knew she had passed, then we learned how she had passed. Each phase had its own things to do, and people to talk to. We have done a lot but don't have all that much to show for it yet. Maybe today will be a turning point."

Maybe it would be. Barb's optimism encouraged me like it usually did. Putting these pieces together was hard, and it was clearer than ever that we were better as a team. It was another reminder of why this community was so important to me. The magic of this island, offering me exactly what I needed, when I needed it, was not lost on me. Barb and Tripp were just as invested in solving this mystery as I was. I was lucky to have friends who took on my challenge as their own. Very lucky.

For the first time in a long time, the ferry was relatively empty. Our footsteps were loud as we climbed the metal stairs to the top boat deck. Even though we were the only passengers on this level, we sat close together and kept our voices low. You never know who could be listening and we both did not want to be the source of island gossip. Parts of stories can spread like wildfire on a dry summer day in a tight-knit community like this.

The ride gave us a chance to bounce our theories off each other. We both were having trouble emotionally getting beyond the coincidence of Charles dating two people with untimely deaths—with at least one being a homicide. As two single women, we talked through how we would figure out the real character of someone we could potentially date. It didn't seem as easy as it used to be, when we were younger, and people were connected through school, family, or some social activity. We both acknowledged the anonymous way people met digitally could keep people from being authentic for longer.

"That is not on my horizon ... at all ... I mean I have zero interest, I am not ready, and I don't know when or if I will ever be ready, but ..." I paused. Barb asked a good question to consider as it related to the case. How do you vet someone you met randomly, through a dating app, or in real life? I continued, "Hypothetically, of course, due diligence would be really important to me. I think I would ..."

"Due diligence?! What?" Barb laughed, "Is this an investment analysis or a date we're talking about?"

I cringed. "Told you I'm not ready."

"Noted, clearly noted." She smiled at me. "But I think you'd have to rely on your own instincts as well as feedback from people you trust. Right? I mean, I could see us discussing a dinner date or a phone call we had with someone we are interested in. Then, I could see us getting a reality check. We would tell each other honestly if someone sounded like a good match for us. We would do that for each other. Don't you agree?"

"Although it is hard to imagine happening, I completely agree. I would want you to do that, I would value your honesty. If the shoe were on the other foot, I would have to be honest with you because, in my heart, I want you to be happy and treated well. It would be really hard to do it alone if you are talking to someone who wasn't connected to your network in any way."

She sighed. "Ultimately, this is the missing piece then, right? Why didn't Carrie feel like she could have these conversations with her closest friends? Why do they know almost nothing about Charles?

Can it be that none of them wanted to make sure he was legitimate and a good guy?"

"Sadly, there are so many things about this that feel wrong on so many levels," I said quietly, more to myself than to Barb.

Once docked, we made our way quickly to The Half Hitch. The small store was bursting at the seams. There was a line of customers waiting somewhat impatiently for their coffee, seemingly engrossed in the screens they held in front of them while fidgeting, swaying, and occasionally glancing up to take stock of the wait. The line snaked to the side of the shop, and we took our place at the end. It moved faster than we anticipated. In a few minutes, we made our way to the street corner, with many of the storefronts and restaurants in our view.

I saw the bright orange enormous tote bag before I focused on the woman whose shoulder it was hooked on. Elbowing Barb and pointing to the person standing in the middle of the street, in front of the coffee shop, I said, "It's her, isn't it? It's Galina, right?"

The tall man standing in front of me turned around so quickly that his messenger bag slightly swung away from his hip. "Galina the resume writer? Yeah, that's her. Are you meeting her here? She's amazing. Found my new job only two weeks after she reformatted mine. Good luck to you!"

"Thank you, that's good to hear," I answered vaguely.

"I'll hold our place, you go. Go and see if she will talk to you. Maybe we can head over to The Captain's Deck or a bench or ..." I didn't wait for Barb to offer other suggestions. I called to Galina, who turned and smiled warmly. Relief, curiosity, surprise, and all the emotions of the last few days all bubbled up at once. However, I had the presence of mind to smile back and approach her like a potential client, just like the man in front of us thought I was.

"Galina, hi! I'm Carr. I grabbed your card from the community board inside the coffee shop. Your work comes highly recommended. Do you have a minute or two to chat?" I extended my hand, which she firmly shook.

"Lovely to meet you, I do have time now, but the store is so crowded, we likely won't get a seat. There is a little cafe a few doors down. Are you good to head there?"

I waved to Barb, encouraging her to join us. "Galina, this is my friend, Barb." They also shook hands, but I sensed a subtle shift in Galina's demeanor, as if she was suddenly a little curious, maybe even slightly guarded. Interesting.

"We had mentioned trying out the cafe for takeout but decided to hold off for tonight. This will give us an opportunity to get a taste of their offerings." I was trying to make small talk, but admittedly, I found myself scrambling. The crowd, the unexpected windfall of Galina appearing right where we needed her to be, the complete randomness threw me and I had to get my head in the game.

"I work by appointment only, I have a few minutes now, but I will have to run soon." Galina smiled sweetly as we settled at a table near the front of the Harborside Cafe. It also was a small shop, but its sunny yellow decor made it seem bigger and brighter. Barb slid into the blue upholstered booth, and I followed her. Galina sat across from us, her tiny frame looking even smaller in the booth's high back and deep cushions. In retrospect, my seat selection was likely a missed opportunity for me to lower her guard. Maybe it would have felt less like an inquiry or a pile-on if I had sat with her. Maybe this started us on the wrong foot.

As the server brought a basket of warm bread knots for us to nibble as we ordered our drinks, my stomach rumbled in response, remembering the last thing I ate was a handful of berries at Dan and Poppy's house. That seemed like days ago. "I'm afraid we won't have time for all this," Galina said as she collected our menus and handed them back to the staff. "How about coffee all around?" That settled that. Galina left no room for misinterpretation.

She had a no-nonsense vibe. "Now, how can I help? Is it you who needs resume services? Or you?" Galina pointed to each of us as her large eyes took stock of us. Galina wore bold patterns, bright colors, and big, chunky rings and bracelets that rattled against the table in front of her.

"Well, we can both use your help," I quickly answered.

"You're both looking for work? Are you co-workers? Caught in a reduction in force? Tell me what's happening, because these tidbits will help change how we approach your projects. Are you aware I also help with social media posts and cover letters? My services range from ..."

Barb jumped in, "Actually, we are working on a project of a different kind. However, we still need your help."

Galina leaned back, flattening herself against the wall of the booth. "What is that supposed to mean? I offer career services—and am not really interested in other kinds of projects." She spoke through tight lips, each sentence ending abruptly. "Who are you really? I recognize your name and your voice—you left me those messages. Now you bump into me, 'coincidentally'. Are you stalking me?"

Nothing lit Barb's fuse faster than unhelpful people with bad attitudes. Check and check, on full display there at the Harbor Side Cafe.

"Stalking you? Are you kidding me right now? We are just trying to ask you a question or two. That is—"

All of sudden we were traveling down a road that would likely come to a dead end.

"Galina, it certainly isn't our intent to make you uncomfortable. You're right, I did leave you a few messages and had hoped to connect with you. We live on Mongin Island, and we recently met a woman who I think you know, too." I waited for her to answer; she waited for me to continue.

"We met a woman named Carrie Nichols, from Atlanta. She's a little taller than me and has blonde hair, too. I think you met her at The Half Hitch on Monday." It was as if Galina's senses failed her—she didn't seem to hear, see, or be able to speak.

"I know you meet a lot of people. Let's see, well, Carrie was wearing a blue top and had a straw hat with a wide blue ribbon and ..."

"Just like her, to wear something that would draw all eyes on her. That hat ... ridiculous. Did she think she was going to the Derby? Look around, do you see anyone else dressed like that? That woman always needed to be the center of attention."

My eyes went right to Barb, but I couldn't tell if she heard what I heard. Galina just referred to Carrie in the past tense. Was it a clue? My heart started to beat a little faster, but I tried to mirror Barb's blank face.

"How do you know Carrie? Do you also live in Atlanta?"

"Carrie, well, she has been in my life for a long, long time. We used to work together, years ago. She worked in the accounting department, and I worked in talent acquisition, which was part of HR at the time. We didn't work on a lot of projects together but now and then our paths would cross."

She looked at her watch and continued, "I have another appointment, so we are going to have to move this along. To answer your question, no, I don't live in Atlanta, thankfully. It's too loud, too crowded, I've relocated."

"To where?" Barb asked almost before Galina's last syllable was spoken.

"To ... why do I need to tell you?" she shot back.

Even though I thought I knew the answer, I asked anyway. "Are you lucky enough to live here? We love living close to the water, there is so much to do here."

She eyed me suspiciously, "What is it that you want? Why do you care about my relationship with Carrie? What's this about?"

I remembered and implemented one of Julie's interview strategies, I said nothing and waited.

"My husband and I moved to Florida a little over a year ago," Galina finally said. "My husband travels to this area every few weeks for some of his investment work, so I tag along. Now that I am an entrepreneur, I can work from anywhere."

"So, you just happened to bump into Carrie? Here at a random coffee shop? Miles away from where you both live? That's an amazing coincidence," Barb challenged her.

"I didn't say I bumped into her, you said that. Our meeting was not impromptu, it was on our calendars."

"Were you helping her with her resume? Was she looking for a new role?"

"No, not that I am aware of, I don't think she is job hunting. I think she is husband-hunting," Galina said, nodding her head for emphasis. Her long, straight hair swung as well, emphasizing her point.

It was impossible to figure out if Barb was thinking the same thing I was. The indifference on her face masked her thoughts. "Why do you think that? Did she tell you that?"

"I told you, I've known Carrie for a long time. I know how she works, but in this case, her mother told me."

"Her ... mother? You know her mother?" I was having trouble wrapping my head around this. Aside from expressing their concern for Carrie's mother or ways they could help her, no one else had mentioned her. Now this person who dropped into Carrie's life for just a few minutes was gabbing away with Carrie's mom?

She looked at her watch again and sighed. "Look, it isn't complicated. I had an important message I needed to deliver to Carrie. Her mom helped facilitate that. It's not hard, right? We met for coffee, I gave her the message and we went our separate ways. No big secret, nothing to figure out. There, that's the end of it."

It didn't feel like it was the end of it. Rather, it felt like I was just getting started. "I know you have to move on to your next appointment. But I'm still not sure how you connected here."

"Well, I am not sure why I need to tell you. Why are you so interested? It's none of your business. I don't owe you an explanation."

"It kinda is our business, more than you would guess, actually," Barb answered.

"Galina, unfortunately, Carrie has had some difficulties since you last saw her," I started. In my peripheral, I saw Barb raise her eyebrow. I knew I would hear about my unusual word choice at some point. I could almost hear Barb say, "Talk about the understatement of the year!" and she would be right.

For her part, Galina did not seem the least bit affected by Carrie's 'difficulties'. I continued, "Sometime after you met on Monday, Carrie became quite ill."

"Hmm, that's really a shame. You never know about these viruses, lots of things going around," Galina answered as she scooted out of the booth, straightened her dress that clung to her legs, and reached over to grab her orange tote. "Please do give her my best."

"Galina, please," I reached gently for her arm, but she jumped back, away from me. Immediately withdrawing my arm, I said, "I will walk with you. I need just a few more minutes with you."

She threw some money on the table but didn't answer me. In a flash, she was out the door. I barely noticed that Barb stayed behind to settle our bill. Standing on the sidewalk, Galina and I were face to face when she said, "I have to go, I can't give you what you want."

I wondered what it was she thought I wanted. There were so many questions I wanted to ask her, but I felt her slipping away from us. Standing there, near the dock, surrounded by strangers, I made the decision to buy time with her. "Listen, come to the island tomorrow. Come, talk to us there. I have things to ask you and I'm sensing there are things you also want to know. If that doesn't work, I can meet you here, but I think it is best if you come to Mongin. You can get your questions answered. There are people I would like you to meet, and we will have a private place to talk. I own a store there and we can sit quietly. I'll text you the ferry schedule and we can pick you up right from the dock. Will you do that? Will you finish this conversation?"

"Text me the schedule, I will let you know." She turned and disappeared into the crowd. I would never be able to determine how many minutes passed before Barb appeared at my side.

"Carr, my friend, I think we just found our turning point."

Chapter 17

"Sorry, but that woman rubbed me every bit the wrong way." Barb's words snapped me out of the word bubble I was in, trying to commit it all to memory. "Now what? Want to sit down and regroup?"

"Let's order our dinners and get back to Mongin. I'm exhausted, you must be too. We still have to go to the cottage and then regroup with the team. Feels like this will be a marathon day and a very long night."

Neither Justin nor Kendra were at The Captain's Deck. We were not as disappointed by their absence as I thought we would be. Now that we were here, and in it, we realized there wasn't more they likely could have told us anyway. Their absence allowed us to talk through what happened in the last hour ... which all seemed surreal. I often think about how Barb and I find ourselves in these extraordinary circumstances, entirely different from any aspect of our day-to-day lives. In reality, we are average people usually doing ordinary things. But now ... one day we're at the chili cook-off and then we're standing at the mainland ferry landing trying to process the intersection of two women we barely know.

We sat at one of the street-side tables Justin had previously suggested and sipped on ice-cold sweet tea. "This is like my tenth drink of the day," Barb said. "I'm going to be sloshing around at this rate." She squeezed a lemon slice over her tea.

"I'm running on fumes," I said. "I need food. How about some of those pretzel bite appetizers I saw that other table order? That should soak up some of the coffee and tea we just guzzled." She laughed with me and just like that we were back to our ordinary, regular life.

With food and drinks to restore us, we wasted no time dissecting our Galina meeting while we waited for our to-go order of sandwich platters. "So, you're not a fan?" I asked Barb.

"Ha, no, not a fan. Couldn't even pretend with Galina. It was just her whole vibe, her whole, I don't know what you call it ... her whole, you know." She leaned back in her chair, raised her left shoulder, and crinkled her nose. "You know, you felt it too. It was her I'm-better-than-you snooty secretive thing. Seems to me she was working very hard to look like she couldn't care less."

I had to agree. "But who is she? What did they have to meet about and why is she talking to Carrie's mother? Weird! The entire thing is so weird."

"It's not exactly like we can randomly call Carrie's mom now and ask about Galina George. The woman just lost her daughter. I don't think we should bother her with this."

"No, I agree, that will be something Julie needs to do if she decides it's relevant. Maybe we can get Galina to tell us if she speaks to us again."

"Do you honestly think she will come to Mongin? I mean, I wouldn't. I don't think she is going to respond to you. Why should she? What does she have to gain?"

"I'm giving it a 50-50 chance, hard to say, right? In the end, she didn't tell us anything, I think what she didn't say is more powerful than what she did share. The only thing is ... if she was involved in Carrie's death, she may want to know what we know. There hasn't been any news coverage, she has no way of knowing what happened and where an investigation currently stands. I can't figure out what possible message she would have to deliver to Carrie, here, while she is on vacation? You need to tell her something so urgently you need to meet in person, after not working together for years? What is that message?"

"Good luck with that! As you say, she wasn't giving an inch! Ohh that woman, she is like a splinter, rubbing you the wrong way."

"Well, the only thing is, now that we made contact, she knows that if we found her, the police can find her too. If she has something to hide, she may want to seem helpful, maybe to throw us off her trail."

"Helpful? We're still talking about Galina, right?"

I sighed, "I know, I know. I already owe you a pie since I lost our Tripp bet. How about double or nothing? I bet you she will come to Mongin."

"You're on. I think you're going to be keeping Miss Lucy plenty busy with all the pie you will be buying me! I think there is zero chance, less than zero chance—basically a negative chance that woman will be on Mongin Island tomorrow or any other day."

"You're on!" We shook on it as two brown shopping bags filled with our take-out order were delivered to our table.

We were soon in the queue for the next Mongin ferry. It felt so reassuring to see a few of our neighbors heading home with us. That feeling of leaving worries on the mainland was never lost on me, even as we carried the weight of this investigation. There were still things we were leaving behind as the water soon separated us from the crowds, the lines, the hustle and bustle. As we reached the top deck, Helen waved from the back bench seat. Against the stark white seat, her copper hair shined in the sunlight. "There you two are! I had no idea you were coming to the mainland today. I was thinking about you earlier, haven't seen you in days. Is Tripp at the store?"

There was an unspoken understanding between Barb and me, that we would keep the conversation light. "We had a few errands to run and picked up something for dinner. How about you? How's your week going?" I asked, silently hoping to avoid Helen's usual probing questions that insisted on answers.

The door was open for Helen to share the various inconveniences and less desirable circumstances she had encountered since we last saw her. Fortunately, there were only a few things that didn't sit well with her and then she moved onto her favorite topic—her book club selections and their schedule of events for the rest of the year. Exploring their choices, coordinating their meeting dates with the store's event calendar, and hearing her ideas for each meeting helped the time pass quickly. Helen gave her heart to this club. It was her way of building community and I tried to focus on her positive contribution, even when—or more accurately—especially when Helen was quick to point out the things she felt negatively affected the island residents.

The boat had just passed my favorite part of the trip, the curve in the land where Mongin was in full sight. Knowing I was almost home, I couldn't help but relax a little. Seeing the tree-lined coast, the miles of beach, and the dock getting closer, my spirits lifted. "So, what's really going on?" she asked as we were almost to the ferry landing.

"With Carrie?" I asked. Helen didn't suffer fools, there was no point in stalling.

"With all of it, yes, Carrie and her friends. They are still in the cottage, but no one has seen them. I brought over food yesterday, but no one answered the door. I heard them in there, could hear them walking around on those hardwood floors, the TV was on. They were in there, but I just left them a cooler bag by the front door. They are on the island until tomorrow? You don't think one of them had something to do with all this, right?"

Barb looked over at us, once again engaged in the conversation. "Helen, believe it or not, it is still too soon to tell who did what to whom. Even after all the work we have done and all the thought Carr has put into this, we don't have the answers yet. Yes, they are planning to leave tomorrow. We are on our way there now, also bringing food. Funny how when all else fails, we feed each other."

Helen agreed, "It's what Miss Lucy does. Week by week, sometimes day by day, she bakes her pies, muffins, and all her treats, often based on what someone wants or needs. Baking is part of the language she speaks with us, for sure a part of the way she cares for all of us. I am so glad Hetty made space for her to sell her goods at the General Store. Her pies have become part of the island culture now."

I sighed slightly. "Those ladies came for a vacation and instead, their lives changed. Things will never be the same for them, that's for sure. Likely, there will be many people on this island who won't forget them anytime soon either." We could all agree on this too.

I continued, "We've learned a lot in the last few days, but to me, there are still a lot of unanswered questions and things that don't make a lot of sense. Rest assured, Helen, we are working on it."

Helen eyed us curiously, taking stock of us, trying to tell if we were speaking the truth. "Hmm, well, I don't know what all that means. You either know things or you don't. I hope you get some resolution soon. We need things to go back to normal. Although, at this point, it's getting harder and harder to determine what that normal is. That's for sure." With that, she carefully made her way down the boat's staircase, crossed the gangplank, and headed off to her cart waiting in the parking lot.

On the short ride to the resort, we drove in companionable silence, as if we were both recharging our social batteries and preparing for the possibilities in front of us. My mind was stuck on the circumstances of Galina and Carrie's meeting. In the absence of fact, my imagination provided dozens of possibilities. My guesses weren't all that helpful ... yet. Progress was slow, but there was still progress.

"Seems like everyone connected to Carrie tells us only what they want us to know. Everyone is protecting something. We need someone's wall to crack just a little so we can figure out how some of these random things are connected," I told Barb.

"That may be true, but I still can't get beyond the amazing coincidence of Charles' dating 'luck'. Something seems very wrong there."

Ready or not, we had arrived. It felt like we were walking along a path on a foggy day, with only a few steps of clarity in front of us. The rest of the path swirled with mixed messages, half-truths, and stonewalled silence. Annabelle sat on the screened porch and called to us as we parked.

"I was wondering if we would see you before we left. Let me get the door and we can catch up." She disappeared into the cottage and reappeared a minute later on the front steps. "I think Mary Frances is resting. I will see if she can visit with you. Either way, you're welcome to hang out with me."

"Is Tracy here?" Barb asked.

"She is. She's in her room. We've all been co-existing here. Aside from a walk around this road with all the cottages, I don't think we've left these walls. Certainly haven't gone to the beach, that's for sure."

"I don't imagine you would, no. It does look like you could survive another few weeks without leaving," I said, sizing up the cakes, breads, and casserole dishes that lined the kitchen counters. "Not sure you need this. We brought some sweets and snacks. There are also a few things for dinner." I held up our bag of treats, which she graciously took and started to plate for us.

"I will save the dinner for later, but we can munch on your snacks. Let me see if the girls can join us." She disappeared down the small corridor, heading toward the bedrooms.

"It is always so strange to me that even after we experience something so traumatic, the mundane tasks of life continue," Barb said quietly to me as we waited.

"For me, doing these small things felt like a victory. Many days, I wouldn't have been able to do even that. I hardly remember those first days."

Renting one of these cottages gave visitors more space than a standard hotel room—which usually translated to people arriving with more vacation stuff—clothes, sporting goods, food, and beach toys. All those extras meant it took a while to pack up. Barb liked to help people plan the business of getting luggage and supplies to the ferry landing as well as all the details of checking out. Knowing Barb, she would take extra care of this group.

"Carr, Barb, so nice of you to visit us before we leave tomorrow." We heard Mary Frances before we saw her. The three of them entered the kitchen. They clearly had not been sleeping, and each of them had those gray tones of exhaustion, sadness, and anxiety woven into their complexions.

Instinctively, we switched gears from being visitors in their home to caring for them. They sat on the woven stools lining the island. Barb and I were busy for a few minutes opening cutlery drawers, finding napkins, pouring drinks, and emptying food containers, pausing on the tasks at hand to watch them as they settled in front of us. It was the empty stool closest to the wall that tugged at my heart, the one where Carrie should have been sitting.

Barb walked through some of the logistics for the next day. Annabelle interrupted, "We packed Carrie's stuff after the police went through her room. I don't think they found anything interesting there, but they did take a few things. They said they would return them, but we don't have them yet."

Mary Frances pushed her plate away from her and folded her arms in front of her. "I think we would all want to know what you and Deputy Julie know. Tell us what happened to Carrie. We are leaving tomorrow. I don't know what else to tell her mom. I think we all need to know where things are and how it all happened."

"Julie said she has been updating you, right? She has all the clinical information and—"

"Please do not tell us more about this rosary pea. It's all we've heard, all we've read about. We can't possibly learn any more about this." Tracy put an end to recounting Julie's areas of focus.

"Let's talk about Charles, we've learned quite a bit in the last few days." They listened silently to our download of Carrie and Charles' time together, but Barb paused as we started to talk about the Tuesday breakfast date. I knew we had to cover this information delicately because we were describing the last few hours of Carrie's life.

"Sounds like Carrie really liked him, maybe he would have been, you know … the one," Tracy said so softly that I wasn't totally sure those were her exact words. She went and stood in front of the big family room windows, still within earshot but with her back walling her off from us. "I should have done more, or maybe, really I should have done less." It was hard to tell, but I think she had begun to cry.

I decided to skip over Poppy and Dan's commentary, knowing that the price to pay for them to hear it far outweighed the information they would receive. The cottage was silent and still for a few minutes while we gave them space to process what they had heard so far. But there were things we needed to know. If we were going to help them, we needed to start getting answers.

There was no good time to push them. "Tracy, I need to know why you have Carrie's computer password," I blurted out, ripped the bandage off, and said it so quickly I saw Barb's head jerk back.

"She has all our passwords, she's our official tech support," Annabelle answered for her.

"So, then I have to ask, why didn't you tell us more about what was on Carrie's computer? Didn't you read her messages, weren't you curious when she went missing?" I continued. "It seems like that would have been step one in a long line of things to do when trying to help find your friend."

Mary Frances gasped. "Read our messages? No way, that was part of the deal. We all said that we would never ask Tracy to snoop around on each other. We all made that promise. It is hands-off unless we ask her for that help."

"I've always been interested in computers, and technology. It comes easy for me, and I help them when they need it. A promise is a promise, I gave them my word. I didn't know Carrie was dead. What if she came back and I stuck my nose in all her business? She would have never forgiven me."

Could it be that simple? There is something about the way Tracy communicates that makes it challenging to believe her. The words were logical but her tight lip, her creased brow, and her explosive statements made me question her.

Annabelle brought Tracy her drink and returned to the island. "Tracy is our tech support. Mary Frances is our librarian, always recommending a good next book. I am the group's sommelier, and Carrie is our bargain hunter, our shopping queen. She always knows where a good sale is, or a special offer or ... well, Carrie *was* good at those things and so many other things, too."

Barb said, "The gift of long-time friendships, right? You all know how to help each other."

"Except for me," Tracy said, "I didn't know how to reach Carrie. I was just frustrated she wasn't doing what I wanted her to do on my vacation. It was all about me. It's awful, I can't believe I acted this way. The last words, the last days were so not what they should have been, because of me, and I'm going to have to live with that."

The room was quiet again, but this time not nearly as comfortable. I think Barb and I were both trying to decide where to go with this introspection, but I sensed we both were willing to move Tracy down on our list of suspects—but not off the list. Their collective explanation seemed to make sense and their group transparency may have been authentic. Admittedly, it was plausible.

Eventually, a few long minutes later, I began again. "As you know, Julie has some things she is exploring, but as a group, we are working on learning how this happened, how Carrie came in contact with rosary pea, and we are meeting up with Julie shortly. There is one more update we want to share with you."

Looking at Annabelle and Mary Frances, I wasn't sure how much more they could absorb. They were fading fast. "After lunch with Charles on Monday, Carrie had an appointment to meet a woman for coffee at a shop nearby. Supposedly, Carrie used to work with her, years ago. We met this woman briefly and she said they worked for the same company but in different departments. I guess they didn't work on a lot of projects together. I know you all don't work together for the same companies, so this is probably pretty unlikely for you to know a former colleague of Carrie's, but did she ever mention a woman named Galina?"

Tracy's glass slipped from her hand and cracked into dozens of uneven, jagged pieces on the dark hardwood floor and Annabelle let out her own gasp. In the commotion, Mary Frances spoke purposefully, with an intensity from deep inside, something we had not seen before. "Are you trying to tell us ... are we to believe that Carrie saw Galina George on Monday?"

Chapter 18

It felt like we were looking through the lens of a kaleidoscope and all the colors had just shifted, showing us a completely different picture than the one we were looking at moments ago.

"Galina, yes, Galina George. She and Carrie spent some time together on Monday. You've met her? You know her?" The words poured from me as I tried to figure out what we missed.

"What did Galina tell you?" Mary Frances asked. Barb and I exchanged a look, the one where we both knew we had stumbled onto something. Barb's right eyebrow arched, and I knew we were thinking the same thing, itching to get to the bottom of this.

Barb answered first, "To be honest, she didn't tell us much. How do you know her?"

"Why do you think she was meeting with Carrie?" I finished.

"Galina and Carrie used to work together, yes that's true. But I don't think Carrie had seen her in years. At least, I was not aware of it. Carrie had not mentioned her in a long time. Years ago, they had some disagreements, but we don't know anything else." When she and Annabelle locked eyes, some message passed between them, but they didn't offer it to us. What were they hiding?

"Mary Frances, I think we all know you know more than that. Something about this news is obviously very troubling. Please, anything you share could help us get to the bottom of all this. Tell me about their disagreements, were they friends at one time?"

Annabelle shut that down, right away. "No, not hardly. They absolutely were not friends."

We waited, in silence, even though it was extraordinarily difficult to be patient. Finally, Mary Frances gave us something. "To be honest, Carrie ended up changing jobs, she left that company. Things got so bad between them that she left. Galina had an ax to grind with Carrie, and you might think her grievances were entirely justified. Most people do. But all of it was getting in the way of her reputation, and Carrie moved on. It took years for that to happen. It was just shocking to hear Galina's name, after all these years. I thought we had heard the last of Galina George a long time ago."

Mary Frances was a smart woman, so she had to know that this was not nearly enough to mean anything. It just was another hoop to jump through. "Grievances about what?" Barb asked directly.

"We don't know the full story, we only know Carrie's side of things and of course, as her friends, we believed her," Mary Frances started.

"That doesn't mean we agreed with everything she did." Tracy, who was on her hands and knees, sweeping the broken glass into a dustpan, finally spoke. "We always said there was more to the story than what Carrie would share."

"Yes, Tracy, which was why we supported her finding a new relationship, which has been a long journey." Annabelle's frustration echoed in every syllable she spoke.

"Ultimately, it is likely why none of us asked her about these dates, this relationship, or what she was doing in her personal life. Come on, you have to admit, none of us really wanted to know if it was all starting again." Mary Frances silenced all of us with that simple statement. "Tracy, it is why you were so angry, you wanted it to be right and for her to be happy, of course. But you also didn't want the possibility of it all starting again. It certainly was a lot easier if Carrie was just casually dating people or if she was just single. None of us would have to go through all that again. Right?"

Barb broke the silence, "All of what?"

Mary Frances looked at her friends, maybe silently asking approval or permission to share something they had each carried for a long time.

"This can't hurt Carrie anymore, Mary Frances. Her pain, her heartache, it's over," Annabelle quietly encouraged her. With one last look at Tracy, who lowered her eyes to the floor, and a deep, long sigh, Mary Frances began.

"It's messy and not at all what Carrie had thought it was or would be. Carrie was young, vulnerable, and I guess naive. But she was also beautiful and smart." Once Mary Frances decided to begin this story, it was clear she wasn't going to stop. She paused only to take a sip of the water in front of her. "Carrie was in a relationship with Andrew George, Galina's husband. It started casually, working together on projects. Work friends, and for a long time, it was just that. But it didn't end there, that's for sure."

"Carrie was in a romantic relationship with Galina's husband?" I repeated, slowly weighing each of Mary France's words.

"She was so inexperienced and young for her age, he absolutely should have known better," Annabelle jumped in. "He hunted her down, she wasn't on his team, but he moved people around, reorganized her department and she ended up reporting to him."

"Wait a minute, they all worked together? Andrew George worked at the same company?" Barb asked, trying to catch up to the words that were quickly filling the room with a whole new dynamic. "Was he her boss?"

"It didn't start that way, but ultimately yes. She started on one project team, and gradually, they ended up working together and eventually she was moved into his organization. He was an executive so Carrie wasn't his direct report, but he took a lot of interest in her, given her level. I don't remember all the things that happened. Do y'all track with the timeline? It just always was just out there, it seemed to go on forever."

Tracy shook her head, "No, remember at first it wasn't any big deal? There were just more projects, additional responsibility, and exposure. Carrie was loving all the new work, the praise, and the recognition. She felt there was a path for her, a path to a promotion and more money. Remember all the dinners where we celebrated her success? None of us thought anything was wrong, at first, and well, for a long time, maybe nothing was. We just thought she was busy at work and didn't have time or energy for herself. Remember?"

"That's true, we were all so excited that she was happy at work and things were going well. She had struggled in her first job out of college and didn't have much confidence—so it was fun to see her growth. She was getting bonuses, and trips for reaching her goals, remember the watch she got? That super expensive one?" Annabelle asked.

"That was when I knew something else was going on. That just doesn't happen anymore, people don't get rewards like that, usually. You might get a gift card or something small for a job well done. Gone are the days of extravagant gifts for the type of projects Carrie worked on and the company she worked for. That was a red flag for me, the big clue, so to speak. And shortly after, we had that big blow-up with her, remember?"

"You mean the 'intervention', Mary Frances? That's what Carrie always called it, whenever we talked about that day," Tracy chimed in.

"Yeah, some intervention." Mary Frances rolled her eyes and shook her head quickly, as if just talking about it was bringing it all back to life in front of her. "She didn't want to hear what we said, and by that time she was in it so deep. We told her, remember? Once we found out he was still married ... I mean, that blew us all away. She had always been so serious about cheating and lying, and there she was—the other woman, trying to justify her actions, telling us we just didn't understand."

She took a deep breath and went on, "We told her this guy had no intention of leaving his wife, no matter what he said. He wasn't going anywhere. It was all the classic things cheaters always say. Andrew said the marriage was over, they just had to 'go through the paperwork, which was going to take time. He and Galina supposedly lived separate lives. Carrie 100% believed every word he said, and her finances, the raises, the bonuses depended on that fact."

Tracy jumped in, "Until we found out that they were still living in the same house, still vacationing together, still were a part of the community, serving on boards, out and about at different events, together. He was some big executive, being praised for his community involvement, service, and leadership. Meanwhile, Carrie was sitting alone, in her condo, waiting around for him to pick her up, which he of course almost never did. A thousand excuses later, he never picked her over his wife. Ohhh how I wanted to shake some sense into her. It's making me mad just thinking about all the times we told her how she was being used."

"That was heartbreaking when Carrie finally realized it. How many years were they together? It was after she left the company, they were still together for at least a year after that. Right? It was at least one more year, so I think it was close to three or four years from start to finish when they were romantically involved. She was devastated, and humiliated, her trust was broken. She made us swear we would never tell her mom and dad. That's how you know, right? A family as close as hers, that's how you know. If you have to keep a secret, something is wrong, like really wrong. I don't think she ever told either of them. At least, not that I am aware of, I should say." Annabelle looked back and forth between Mary Frances and Tracy for confirmation.

"Probably was a little more than a year or so after she left that company until she finally ended it with him. That night we all met at your house, Annabelle, and she told us it was over, that she was done. We opened that bottle of prosecco you had in your refrigerator. We toasted her, we laughed, we cried, it was everything that night. Every time I think about all that happening, I can still see all the emotion on all our faces. We were relieved that she could move on, that she would finally be free of him. Later, she told us, she told us all that she appreciated how we walked with her on her path even though she knew we all disapproved of it."

Tracy sighed. "We all just wanted the best for her, and the relationship with Andrew was clearly not it. Could be part of the reason we all reacted the way we did to her behavior this week. This was the first time she has been serious about her approach, been intentional, I guess, about dating and she got all head over heels again. Don't you think? Don't you feel like she already used up a lot of grace and patience? I'm going to have to think through this and come to terms with it. As I said, I may never know, I may just have to live with this."

"I'm going to try to get Galina here tomorrow," I said. "If that happens, I know I will have things to discuss with you afterward, to confirm what she says and all. Barb, is there a way to extend their checkout until mid-afternoon? Would you be willing to stay a little longer tomorrow?"

"This cottage is not rented until next week, so from my perspective, we are good. What do y'all say?"

Mary Frances spoke for the group, "I think we will all be willing to stay to help, at least for a few hours. I'm anxious to get home, we've been hanging out here, hoping to help, but I don't think we did much. There are arrangements back home to attend to, Carrie's mom needs us … but a few more hours won't swing things too much, we can do it. Barb, you mentioned the housekeeping has been scheduled for tomorrow morning, right after our stuff is picked up. Can you rearrange everything—the island transportation, the ferry, all of it?"

"I'll take care of everything, consider it done."

Even if we didn't completely understand it then, Barb and I carried the weight of all we learned with us as we climbed into the cart, both of us hoping for some island magic.

Chapter 19

"Whose cart is that?" Barb asked as we pulled into my small driveway. In addition to Tripp's blue cart, someone else was parked in front of my house. "Were you expecting anyone?"

"Miss Carr!" Jacob and Buddy burst from the screen porch and ran down the side steps together.

"Jacob, my friend, what are you up to?" My spirits immediately lifted seeing Jacob and his mom. This week was a blur and I missed visiting with all my neighbors and friends.

"My mom has something for you, and Mr. Tripp has been showing me how to throw a frisbee. Did you know Buddy can catch one, most of the time?" His words all came out at once and his face was filled with the excitement and pride of learning something new.

Katie greeted us from the porch. "Poor Buddy is going to sleep well tonight. Jacob has had him running laps in your backyard!"

We all watched as Jacob tossed the red disc and Buddy dutifully ran after it, his little legs and white paws lifting him off the ground to catch it right before it crashed to the ground. Everyone clapped for the duo, both of whom looked very pleased with their new trick. "Jacob, sometimes Buddy forgets to bring things back that we throw to him. He must really want to play this game with you!" I congratulated him for teaching Buddy something new.

A shadow fell across Katie's face. "Sorry to barge in, but I need to talk to you. Do you have a minute?"

"This sounds serious, is something wrong?"

"Hmm, not wrong. But there is something I need to share with you and Julie. Tripp said y'all had a call later?" she asked as we headed through the screened porch to my kitchen, keeping her voice low. "I don't want Jacob to think there is something he needs to worry about, you know how he is. He hasn't lost his alert for when there may be trouble. No matter how many good things happen, I know there is a part of him that is always looking over his shoulder, watching for danger. I hate that for him."

I smiled gently, knowing she walked with a lot of guilt regarding Jacob's early years and the instability they had in their lives before Mongin. "Katie, you have made a wonderful home for him. Life was hard for you both, and you raised him to be an incredible boy. There are no perfect parents, you know that. There are quite a few things I wish I had done differently with my children. I think most parents feel that way. Time teaches us all."

"When I see him, just being a child like tonight, I feel terrible for how fast he had to grow up, how unsure it all was for most of his life. With my family as it was, I had no idea what I was doing. I had no role models, no one to show me, no one to talk some sense into me. I hate that he had to bear that burden and I can't undo it for him now."

"I talk about that with Meredith and Nicholas, when they tease me about being 'that mom'. You know, the one who had all the rules, who held them accountable, who didn't always speak softly, who had high standards—not the fun parent. It's easy to feel like your parents weren't perfect people—until you have problems in your own family, as everyone does. Then you realize your parents were just people trying their best with what they had on their plates and what they brought from their childhood experiences, which likely wasn't perfect either. No one has it all figured out—and if they tell you they do, they are trying to convince themselves and you!"

I had seen her like this several times before, sliding into a val-
ley from the stress of being a young, single parent, shouldering the
finances, the parenting, the job, life, all the decisions and responsibil-
ities. All this and still being young enough to have her own dreams
that now were put on hold, not knowing if they would be replaced
only with dreams for her son. I wrapped her in the hug I thought she
needed. She didn't resist.

"Jacob is thriving. He is a great student, a wonderful friend. He is
loving and kind. I think you did the very best with all the extraordinarily hard things you faced. I'm just so grateful we all get to watch
him grow and that you share him with us."

"You're like the mom I never had."

"You and Jacob are the bonus family I needed." Her shoulders
relaxed and I waited for her to be ready to share whatever brought
her here tonight. She moved to the opposite side of my kitchen island,
took a deep breath and started, "This might be nothing, and maybe
Jacob has learned to have his antennae up from me … but it doesn't
feel insignificant."

"You have good judgment, Katie. What is it?"

"Since the busy season has officially ended, the resort has cut back
on some of the housekeeping staff and grounds crew, which is totally
fine with me. They promised me a consistent, full-time schedule and
they have kept their word. I like to be busy, makes the day go fast and
I don't have time to worry about all the things going on. If I am busy,
I just focus on my work."

"Me too, that's exactly why I'm a little anxious about the slower
days coming."

She nodded her head, and I saw a flash of understanding that
maybe what she was feeling was not her unique burden. "So last week,
they asked me to take a golf cart and ride around to several locations
on the property. They asked me to change out the garbage can liners
and put fresh ones into the cans near the beach club, the tennis courts,
the cottage road, the fitness trail, and both entrances to the beach.
Some of the other staff have other locations—these were just my
spots. Since there aren't so many visitors, not all these have to be

emptied every day. They said this would be part of my weekly tasks, likely until winter."

She described her tasks in such detail that I could visualize her driving to all the different locations and loading the bags into the flatbed of the cart. However, I was struggling to understand what any of this had to do with me or Julie. "You know that shuttle stop, the one behind the conference center? The one at the entrance to the cottage road?"

I nodded but said nothing.

"Well, I realized today I skipped that one earlier this week. I should have emptied it on Wednesday—I'm scheduled for Mondays, Wednesdays, and Fridays. I have a set route but somehow, I missed it. The can was loaded today, filled right to the top. You know how the resort built the little receptacles around the garbage cans to keep the animals and critters out? Well, I noticed there were a few things on the ground, behind the can, right near the back of the fence. And when I was grabbing those, I found this."

She walked over to the kitchen table on which her white canvas tote was resting. She pulled out a large clear bag that held a plastic cup. A tiny bit of what looked like coffee rested at the cup's bottom. Katie brought it to me and said, "Do you see the coffee shop name on this?"

Turning the bag over, I read the words once to myself and then softly to Katie, "The Half Hitch." The hairs on my arms stood up. Coincidences seemed to be as plentiful as the oyster shells that dotted Mongin's beach.

"Tripp mentioned you and Barb met someone there. I've read a few reviews about that place, but I have never seen one of their cups here, on the resort property. Not in any of the rooms, not in the cans, nowhere. I think I would have remembered since their logo is pretty unique ... And it stuck with me, it was odd that you were just there earlier this week, and then this cup appears—especially in that garbage can, where the shuttle drops off people, mostly visitors. Right? It feels significant. Well, it did to me anyway. You see a lot when you spend time in the guests' rooms."

"Funny enough, I tried to go there again today," I answered vaguely, distracted by the order printed on a sticker on the side of the cup. "This is very interesting," I said slowly. "We need to get to Julie."

Julie answered on the first ring, "Carr, I thought we were doing a video call at 8:00. Did you get the invite I sent earlier?"

"Something's come up, do you have a minute now?"

Julie absorbed everything I relayed to her and she responded as I hoped she would. "I will be there. It's going to take some time for me to get someone from the forensic team to meet me at the boat. We will be there as quickly as possible."

"Good for you for trusting your instincts, Katie," I said as the call ended.

We were interrupted. Tripp, Barb, Jacob, and Buddy filled the kitchen, hungry, hot, and thirsty. Buddy slurped his water, probably splashing more on the floor than into his mouth. Stretching across the kitchen rug, with his small chest rising and falling rhythmically as he caught his breath, he kept his eyes on us, watching for one of his favorite times of the day ... dinner. He came to the right house; we both enjoyed a good meal.

"Barb and I picked up some sandwiches, do y'all want to stay and eat with us?" We were soon setting places for five on the screened porch.

"I will be back in a minute, go ahead and get started, please don't wait for me," I called to them over my shoulder as I returned to the kitchen for my phone. When Mary Frances answered my call, I knew this one piece of information would be easy to get.

"Carr, this is a surprise, everything okay?"

"Sorry to bother you, I know you must be busy packing and likely already had enough of me today. Just a quick question ... on Monday, when Carrie went to the mainland, how did she get back to your cottage? Did y'all pick her up from the ferry?"

"It was our spa day, so unfortunately, we weren't available to pick her up. She took the resort shuttle from the dock. We had a pretty full day at the spa and then we grabbed a treat at Treehouse Coffee. We sat on their porch and chatted with other visitors. Carrie was already back when we all returned. Makeup was off, clothes were changed, and her hair was up in a ponytail. I think she had been back for a while. Tracy may know more—they went for a walk once we got back. They both were pretty restless."

Promising to connect again first thing in the morning, we hung up. Before heading back to the table, I texted Galina the times of the early morning boats and confirmed I would pick her up at the landing. The read receipt meant she saw my message, but she did not respond—infuriating—just as Barb said.

Barb's eyes were on me when I pulled out my chair, but I did not meet her gaze and got busy fixing the food I added to my plate. Katie was right about Jacob. He was sensitive and perceptive. Jacob was also in the middle of a string of knock-knock jokes and had a captive audience around the table. The things we needed to discuss could wait. This moment of being present with these people could not. One or two quick comments would have changed the entire vibe of the dinner. It turns out that Jacob and Tripp each had a pretty big repertoire of silliness, and right now, that was exactly what we all needed. Whether we knew it or not, circumstances would soon be explained, lives already changed would undergo more upheaval— things would never be exactly as they were then, in that moment. The power of laughter and joy, creating these memories felt right and necessary.

"Come on little man, we have a few things to do at home and you need to hit the hay. Bring your plate into the kitchen please and we will head out," Katie said to Jacob. He gathered a few things from the table and brought them into the kitchen. As we followed behind him, everyone carrying plates, utensils, and trays, we caught the last few bits of his conversation with Buddy. "So next time, maybe we can go to the beach, and you can chase the frisbee down the whole side. Would you like that, good boy?"

Buddy wagged in agreement, his flappy ears perked up, at the ready, listening politely. Jacob hugged him and gave him a gentle kiss on his typical Lab blockhead. When Jacob and I compare all the things we love about this dog, we would sometimes debate if Buddy's head was actually shaped more like a triangle than a square block. I smiled to myself, thinking that either way, that head was the perfect place for a kiss. Seeing these two friends together just filled my heart. We were watching Jacob grow, watching him become independent and confident. I meant what I said earlier to Katie, I was grateful she shared him with us.

"Thanks for the fun dinner." Katie reached over for a goodbye hug. "And keep me posted if I can help with what we discussed earlier."

"We'll stay in touch on that. Good night you guys!" We all watched Katie make a quick U-turn and head toward the employee housing only a few streets away. Jacob had crumpled into the cart seat, looking like the activity of the last few hours had all of a sudden drained him. There was no doubt about it, sleep would soon be coming both his and Buddy's way.

Almost before they were out of earshot, Barb needed to know, "What was going on? You learned something, what is it?" Tripp turned toward me to hear better, and we were quickly standing nearly shoulder to shoulder.

"We have work to do. Julie and her team are on the way. Katie found something, that's one thing. Julie needs to weigh in and investigate. We need to do some digging, we need to know more about Carrie and Andrew and ultimately, why Galina and Carrie needed to meet. Once we figure that out, I think the pieces will fall into place."

Chapter 20

Funny enough, we each had a laptop to grab. Barb opened her backpack and fired up hers. She always had it with her to check on work-related reservations, inquiries, emails, and so on. Tripp grabbed the one from his work bag in his cart. He also brought it with him as a back-up to the store's computer and in case he wanted to research something for a customer. I don't think he ever needed it, but Tripp liked to be prepared so he could be helpful. Mine was resting on the bookshelf nearby. I made a large pot of coffee, and we were soon settled at the kitchen table. Buddy snored gently from his cozy rug. Since everyone was in their place, he could sleep peacefully, officially off-duty.

"Look at us, we look like we could be at a late-night college study session!" Barb laughed.

Tripp agreed, "Kind of does feel that way, like we're about to do a group project. Might need some popcorn or snacks or something."

"Remember those air poppers? The hot air poppers? Did you guys have one? It used to be a college dorm room staple, remember those? Made those huge batches of popcorn and we all felt so healthy because it didn't need oil or butter. It was the one thing that could always draw a crowd, that's for sure."

Barb nodded, "Yes, but it actually tasted like the packing peanuts that you put in a box when you mail something. Butter on popcorn is a requirement. I will go down fighting on that fact."

"I think I have snacks, let's see what we can gather up. Today was a crazy eating day, that's for sure. Might as well go out in a blaze of glory."

Instead of settling down to work, we all opened a few cabinets, the pantry door, and the freezer. In no time, we had a miniature buffet of treats. "Guess I haven't outgrown my ability to procrastinate—just like in school when I had a project due!"

"Well, thank goodness for that, this gelato is amazing!" Tripp said. His spoon was already scraping the bottom of his bowl.

As we snacked, Barb made a list of things we needed to know and outlined possible ways we could get answers. Our lighthearted break was over. There were quite a few loose ends and things that didn't make sense. Our list was long and daunting.

"We may not have all the answers before Mary Frances and all of them leave tomorrow. We can't keep them here any longer," Barb said slowly as she reviewed our notes.

"How about I try to learn a little more about Galina's husband, Andrew?" Tripp said. "I can work on that."

"Well, I want to know what brought them to this area so regularly," I said, thinking out loud. "The Atlanta, Florida, Lowcountry connection—I need to understand it. Remember, when we first met Carrie and her friends, I asked them if they had ever been to Mongin. Only Mary Frances had traveled here. None of them had said they had been to the mainland. So, if Andrew is coming here for work, it doesn't sound like Carrie, as his prodigy, came with him."

"We also don't know when these trips started, right? Maybe Carrie was already out of his life," I continued. "What about the money being deposited into her account regularly? That's a question we can ask her friends tomorrow. It's too late to reach out at this hour, but I am adding that to the list of things we need to ask. I think, for now, we all have our areas of focus, at least until Julie arrives."

In a blink, we were back to a new version of our 'study' session. We worked in silence—the only sounds were keys clinking, pens scratching against the yellow legal notepads scattered around the table, and the occasional whoosh of the AC unit working to keep the temperature comfortable.

"Could this be something?" Tripp's words broke the silence of our concentration. "Look at this." His screen had what looked like a hundred tabs opened, but in the foreground was a group photo of five people in formal attire smiling into the camera. Second from the right side of the photo was Galina.

Tripp pointed to the man to Galina's left, "The caption here says this man, the one with the silver hair, this one is Andrew George. The tall man here, in the center, is Jett Jepson."

"Never heard of him, no clue." Barb shook her head.

"Are they at a fundraiser? Mary Frances said Andrew used to go to a lot of charity events. What are you looking at, Tripp?"

Turning his screen around, he explained, "I just searched Andrew's name and then added a bunch of things to the criteria. Got some hits from Atlanta, then some in Florida, but when I added the Lowcountry location, he was featured on the society page of The Island Insider. Looks like they are at this fundraiser for the state senator candidate. Says this event was held on the mainland a few months ago at the Waterside Mansion. You know that place, right? The fancy hotel on the water with its own private dock. It's very exclusive. According to this, it was a $5,000 per plate event. Can you imagine? This wasn't even the kick-off event, just a campaign stop. The money is unbelievable."

"So, Andrew and Galina come to the mainland to attend a fancy political fundraiser for a candidate who is not running in their home state? Why? They must be connected to him in some way. Who is the candidate?" Barb asked without taking a breath.

"Here's a theory ... maybe the connection is not with this candidate," I said as I typed. "Maybe it's with Jett Jepson. He appears to be a political operative, looks like he is a campaign finance manager and strategist. Is Andrew running for office in Florida? How can we find this out?"

"I will keep searching," Tripp decided.

From the corner of my eye, I could see Barb's blue pen rolling back and forth, over and over, between her thumb and the index finger of her right hand. Her eyes were tracking back and forth. Whatever page was open on her screen, it was keeping her attention. And the more it was keeping her attention, the more I wanted to know what it was. "I can't take it. Barb, what are you looking at? All I can see are your eyes going back and forth. You must have found something, what is it?"

"For heaven's sake, Carr, you scared me half to death, what? You must not have found something too interesting yourself if you're watching my eyeballs!"

"Well, that's completely accurate. But also, I can tell you *did* find something, what is it? The suspense is killing me."

"Well, I'm not sure this is much of anything. First, I found an article about Jessica Connors, Charles' other girlfriend who passed away suddenly." Barb casually laced her not-so-subtle opinion of Charles into her description of Jessica.

"The article is in her hometown paper, almost like an extended obituary notice. Seems like Jessica was originally from a pretty small town in North Carolina, and this is a 'local girl meets an untimely death' story. She moved to the big city, to Atlanta, and then passed away, unfortunately. Jessica sounds like she did a lot for the community, sounds like a nice person. They were proud of their hometown girl who did well."

"Shame that she passed so young." Tripp spoke slightly louder than a whisper, so we almost spoke over him. He related to the grief of a loss that felt too soon.

Barb continued, "It's this blog about her that I found. It's so compelling, I feel like I know them personally. Jessica's sister is the author, and she says this is her grief journal, a way for her to write about her road through her loss. She wrote it hoping she would help others on their journey. This is not just a journal of feelings. There is a lot of information here about how she worked through all the phases of dealing with a sudden death in the family. I scrolled through to the end—there have been no new entries for at least four years. So, I haven't read it all, thanks to an impatient person, sitting right here at the table, but …." She looked up and winked at me.

"The first few entries are all about the shock of someone young and healthy passing away. One early post described how Jessica ran a half-marathon just two weeks before. No wonder her family was so shocked, right?" Barb took off her reading glasses and rubbed her eyes.

Scrolling to a later entry, she said, "But get this, Jessica's only sign of illness was some 'stomach' trouble the night before she passed. According to her sister, it was the first time in years that Jessica had been sick—she lived a healthy lifestyle. Basically, at the time this was written, it sounds like the family was having trouble wrapping their heads around the idea that Jessica was fine one day, had this 'stomach bug' the next day, and then died that night. She writes a lot about the unexpected new reality of this special kind of heartache."

Barb broke our silence a minute later, "This line, wow, talk about a gut punch. Listen to this. 'In one phone call from my father, I became an only child, and my parents would never again say they have two children.' I mean, you can tell the grief is raw, right?"

"Are you really thinking Charles was involved?" Tripp asked.

"I don't know what to think. Charles doesn't seem too high on Julie's radar right now. Unless of course, she learned more from the officers and others involved in Jessica's case. Carr, what are your thoughts?"

"To be honest, Charles is pretty unlikeable. Right? He was pretty nasty when I first told him about Carrie. And he seems pretty mercurial, up and down, unpredictable. I want to have compassion for him but just when I let my guard down with him, he says something awful."

They both agreed so I went on, "All that being said, Julie has reminded me that someone's odd behavior or quirky personality doesn't make them a murderer. And in this case, with two women dead that we know of … what does that mean? Serial killer? I don't want to create a false narrative, but the reality is he had no motive to kill Carrie. At the heart of it, I think he did like her and wanted to build a relationship with her."

I took a long drink of my now cold coffee and continued, "I just don't see it. He would wait to meet Carrie in person, here on vacation, and then poison her? Here, where there are so few people on the island, and it is easier to find a suspect, unlike a large metropolitan city? If he wanted to poison her, I would think he would have done it back closer to their home. To me, this doesn't fit. Unless, like you said, Julie has new information."

"So, you're not ruling him out, in your opinion," Barb said. "But you're also not putting him at the top of your suspect list. Am I right?"

"I am leaning that way, yes, but I am not 100% sure of anything right now, to be honest. Let's wait and see what Julie has learned and then we can—"

"She's here now, I just saw headlights through the window." Tripp got up to open the side door.

"Well, I guess we're about to find out what road we will travel," I said.

Chapter 21

My kitchen was filled with Julie, her team, and the several forensic kits they carried.

"Thanks, Tripp. I was just about to knock. Hey, everyone, this is Peter and Sharyn. They work in our forensics unit." After saying hello, she went on, "I want to make sure we get these items tested and properly entered into evidence. Carr, is it okay with you if they set up on your counter, next to your sink?" There was little room for chit-chat. It was clear Julie had an agenda to cover with us.

The officers got busy laying down mats and taking out syringes and chemicals. Suited up in protective gear, they carefully went to work on Katie's plastic bag and The Half Hitch cup. Watching the cup be dusted for fingerprints was a brand-new experience. Next, they carefully extracted some of the liquid and filled various test tubes. Peter and Sharyn were busy testing, observing, and recording results. Who would have thought this would have been happening in my kitchen? The whole night was surreal.

Julie refocused us. "In the interest of time, let me cover a few things quickly. Unfortunately, not much progress on Carrie's landline. She hardly used it and there was no call to or from Galina or Andrew.

Essentially, seems the only calls she got were from telemarketers and politicians."

"The worst!" Barb exclaimed.

"Right?" Julie went on. "But before we get too far down this path, I want to fill you in on Charles."

She pulled out her notebook, which always struck me as surprisingly old-school for someone who was immersed in technology all day long, and flipped through page after page until she landed on one filled with her block handwriting. "The long and short of it is, Charles Anders had nothing to do with Jessica Connor's death. Eventually, it was determined that there was a genetic component, a pre-existing gastroenterological condition likely combined with a previously unknown food allergy. Essentially, Jessica's nephew had a similar medical experience about nine months after her death and they pieced it all together retrospectively. Terrible circumstances, but nothing criminal."

"There goes the serial killer theory," Barb chimed in. "If he had been involved in two deaths, I think it's fair to have wondered if there were more out there somewhere." She waved her hands vaguely in the direction of some other place for emphasis.

Julie studied us briefly but did not explore that idea. We were watching her discover new facts and file them away in some mental database. I knew her well enough to know that she heard and processed everything, missing very little. That comment would stay with her. Even as she said she was dismissing Charles as a suspect, she would not forget something so heavy.

She went on, "All of Charles' story checks out in terms of Carrie, too. He hasn't hidden anything. Believe it or not, we were able to recover the breakfast items from the resort dumpsters. Everything has been tested and it's all clear. Of course, we know that Carrie was poisoned before the breakfast date. Testing the breakfast was just part of the process, leaving nothing to chance. To be clear, we have no motive, no real suspicion, and it just doesn't fit. We have cross-checked everything he told you, Carr, and everything he told us. There are no discrepancies. In the spirit of crossing people off the list, I am reasonably comfortable with eliminating her friends—all of them—as suspects. Have to be honest, at first, I questioned some of what they said, how they acted, and the whole package. But they all check out, weird as some of it is."

We were an attentive audience to Julie's explanations. I could tell that Tripp, Barb, and I had thoughts about it all. Emotionally and physically drained from the days we spent getting to know these people, listening to and digesting their explanations, their backstories, the things they shared, and the things they hid—all of it—left us with the sinking feeling of being in a race where the finish line is somewhere out there, maybe nearby or maybe so far down the road we may not ever find it. There was no clear path here.

The forensic team was done. The samples were drawn and recorded, and the evidence was secure in their kits. They waited patiently, leaning against the counter. Now that they were packed up, I made a fresh batch of coffee and refreshed drinks and snacks.

"I know the team is anxious to get these samples processed. The sooner we get them in, the sooner we will have some information. For all we know, this could be a random cup, thrown away by someone with nothing to do with any of this. Even if it was Carrie's, it could mean nothing. Anyway, we won't stay much longer, but I want to share a few other updates on Carrie's finances. But first, fill me in on what y'all uncovered. You've been busy too."

Each of us took turns updating the group, adding color, but not our conclusions, to each other's words. Julie absorbed everything, listening, writing, nodding, but she asked nothing until we were done.

"We absolutely need to speak to Galina. She knows something but it's anybody's guess what that is. Has she answered you?"

Checking my phone for the hundredth time since I texted her, I shook my head.

"I am going to have officers keep an eye on her, from a distance, of course, but we will make sure she doesn't pack up and leave the mainland. Also, let me call law enforcement in her hometown. If she isn't on the first two early boats tomorrow, we will pay her a visit. I will be here on the island, just in case you need me. If I can't be here, Cole will be here, one of us will be close by."

"One last topic, Carrie's finances. Remember I told you she had all the normal expenses and some savings, a retirement account? Nothing unusual except this structured settlement, this $5,000 a month, every month for years. Right? The money is all just sitting in a low-interest savings account. A deposit arrives at the beginning of the month, but she hasn't touched it once."

Not waiting for an answer, she continued, "This has been one rabbit hole after another and is still a work in progress. The way it looks right now, it *looks* like she is getting regular payments from an agency in Georgia. But nothing about any of this is what it may look like, right? First of all, Georgia, and any other state for that matter, does not send payments through foreign routing and an international account. Also, the sending account is registered to the Georgia Association for Citizens. As you can imagine, such an association doesn't exist. Unfortunately, Carrie was involved in something, and I think we all know it's likely a part of all of this."

Learning more about this payout was something at the top of my list. It felt more critical than even speaking with Galina. Something in the way Julie said it, the mystery, the implication of it all, weighed heavily. The night had a somber, unsettled ending.

Julie started packing up, too. Papers were shuffled, dishes were loaded into the dishwasher, and someone was wiping down the table. This part of the night was over. As they headed out the door, Julie turned back to me. "I'm going to be up thinking through this. And, if I know you at all, I think you will be, too. Text me if you want to talk."

"Sleep? What's that?" I half-laughed. "I want to be 100% ready for Galina if she shows up here tomorrow. I don't want her to throw me off track by talking about something that I know nothing about. I want to talk to her and listen to her answers—not the other way around."

After packing up her car, the team climbed in, waved, and were off. The street was illuminated only by the headlights of Julie's Suburban, which dimmed to almost black in just a few seconds. Barb spoke first, "I don't believe she is coming."

"Galina?"

"Yes, I understand what you said earlier, I get it. I just don't see it."

"You may well be right. I think she is going to want to appear helpful, she is going to want to know what we know. With that in mind, I need to be ready. This is the trouble, right? She may know everything, and we know only some things. How do we get her to tip the scales in our favor?"

"I'm afraid I'm done for the night. I'm sorry to say I can't think straight anymore, but I'm happy to take the first run of the ferry pickup tomorrow if that will help you, Carr." Tripp stifled a yawn as he packed up his laptop.

"Some guests are leaving tomorrow, and I have some last-minute arrivals too. I can probably do an early ferry run but I will be booked most of the day. I hate to leave you like this. Do you need help? What's the plan?"

I hadn't really thought about the plan yet. There just were too many things that happened today to think of any one thing. I shivered in the chilly night air. "Tripp, if you can watch the store tomorrow, I will do the ferry runs. If Galina is on a boat, I will need to just have to play some of this by ear—my very least favorite thing to do. I have some ideas, but what I piece together tonight will determine how this all unfolds. And I'm afraid we have asked Carrie's friends to stay here for nothing. Also, I can't stop thinking about this whole Florida, Georgia, Lowcountry connection and what it has to do with Carrie. I know I won't be able to sleep until I have at least made progress in understanding that, at the minimum. I'm sure Julie is thinking the same—it's the connection. This is at the heart of all of Carrie's story. Understanding that, well, that's what I need. To be honest, the sooner the better."

As Barb and Tripp headed to his cart, she asked the question we all were thinking, "Tomorrow could be the day then, right?"

Chapter 22

Walking into my house and feeling its stillness was like colliding with a brick wall and it hit me hard. Always my haven, these walls protected my family and friends. Its foundation anchored our joy in shared experiences and our time together. Home was where I felt settled and tonight, I expected it to be as it always was. This feeling was so ordinary, so much a part of my life here. Opening the door always was like fitting the last puzzle piece in place.

But tonight, ideas, fragments of conversations, and replays of the day's events raced through me, only pausing briefly to supercharge my heart into pounding a little faster. There were just too many thoughts in my head and too much pressure on the minutes moving me closer to tomorrow without the answers, without knowing what happened to Carrie. The ticking pendulum of the wall clock hanging in my hallway reminded me over and over that morning was coming, hurry, there is so much more to know. If I was going to get anything done, I needed to reset before I lost any more time.

But how? It was late and I was so wired that I knew the standard stress release tricks were way too benign for my state of mind. There seemed to be nothing left for me to offer to this day. But then suddenly, it was there right in front of me. Mongin. The island would deliver what I needed; this place would be all that it always was—my sanctuary. It wasn't just my house, our dream house, filled with the memories of my husband with me, and those of our family growing roots in this home, which connected me here. It was this magical island itself that would soothe me in a way nothing else could.

Suited up with my jacket, flashlight, and reflective leash, Buddy and I headed out to explore the resort roads. We had no specific destination in mind, only to travel one step further from the weight of the day. In the quiet, I felt as if this was only our moment. The tags on Buddy's collar jingled softly as he trotted along. He thoroughly enjoyed the unexpected windfall of a late walk and the opportunity to sniff the creatures who scampered across the roads and watched us from the tree-lined medians. I could see the lights on in some of my neighbors' houses and the colors of TVs that entertained them in their family rooms. I smelled the sea air and heard the waves roaring up our shore. But when we turned onto the main resort road, I finally felt it—the Mongin Island magic, the feeling that connected me to this place on my very first visit so many years ago. The feeling of being exactly where I was meant to be, exactly how I was supposed to be, my peace. I felt protected under the canopies of the tall live oaks that had stood guard over this property for centuries. Like the walls of my house, these trees were the structure of my island home. I was renewed and focused.

Walking through my side door this time, everything was totally different. Home was home again. It was not hurrying me, it did not push me away, it was not filled with anxious thoughts of broken promises or letting people down. I quickly showered, cleaned up, lit my eucalyptus and spearmint candle, and settled back at the kitchen table. The time was now, I was ready.

My laptop screen quickly resembled Tripp's, one window after another stacked on top of each other. Crossing out possibilities, adding new ideas, searching for leads, and reading articles left me with one dead end after another. I grabbed one of the legal pads still on the table from earlier that evening and made some quick notes. As I prepared a list of data I needed to share with Julie, an idea came to me so quickly that I sat back immediately in my chair. Had we been looking at these mysterious deposits and bank information all wrong? My pulse raced. My hands flew across the keyboard.

Bingo. It wasn't the Georgia Association for Citizens. It wasn't a structured settlement from a state lawsuit or program. It actually was the GA Association for Citizens. And when I said it aloud, I knew. The G was for Galina and the A was for Andrew. Digging more, I found the correct foundation, with their names listed on the public documents filed with the state. These indicated they were the registered agents of this foundation. I realized then that the bank account information Julie had was missing the foundation's full name—GA Association for Citizens United for Change. No wonder it wasn't easily found by law enforcement. After sorting through the web of this information, I knew one thing for sure: Carrie was being paid month after month, year after year, from an account tied directly to Galina and Andrew.

Paid for what? And logically the next question would be, why did she never touch this money? There were endless possibilities, all compounded by the reality that the people related to Carrie and this case all behaved similarly—even those closest to her. They answered only the questions asked of them and offered the least amount of information necessary to do so. Andrew was the common factor between Carrie and Galina, so maybe he would be the person who could provide some direction here—even if he didn't know he was doing so.

For being a major metropolitan city, it was surprising and somewhat unsettling to me that a non-celebrity like Andrew would have this volume of news blurbs about him. Granted, many were different versions of the same story, but he either had a very active social media manager or he was connected to newsworthy people. On the surface, his life wasn't so compelling that there should be page after page of search engine hits on his name. Skimming, I ruled out some blurbs and headlines due to the timing, the location, or other obvious filters. Carrie's payments started five years ago. That time frame put me almost a dozen pages into the search results, and that is where it started to get interesting.

Sprinkled among the stories of dinners, golf tournaments, and ribbon-cutting ceremonies Andrew attended either as a representative of his company or as a private citizen, there were lots of hits about projects and deals in which he was involved. I read those stories carefully, looking for the clue crumbs I hoped to use to prepare for tomorrow.

The strain of reading about Andrew's adventures made my eyes sting. Truth be told, I almost quit for the night, hoping to get just a little sleep before my day officially began. But then I saw it—the first few words listed at the bottom of almost the last page of results. So far down, it would have been easy to miss, but something had pushed me to finish reading everything I could find, and I knew immediately that this story was different.

"Local Atlanta Executive, Andrew George, Supports Budding Entrepreneur" was linked to a story about Andrew purchasing three homes at the end of a cul-de-sac nestled in a community north of the city to help launch a high-potential business venture. I didn't know the specific neighborhood, but I was familiar enough with the general area to know these homes were in an up-and-coming suburb. A quick search on a real estate site confirmed the sales price and now, the property value slightly over five years later. My questions bubbled up faster than I could type. Who was the entrepreneur and why did he need three houses? How did Andrew know him? The timing worked, but did this have anything to do with Carrie?

That last question was answered first. Embedded in the story was a photo of Andrew and Miguel Rosa, the founder of Rosa Bakery Imports. Mr. Rosa's business focused on providing Central American food services and products to the booming local restaurant scene. Atlanta is filled with foodies who have an appetite for authentic, culturally diverse, and interesting offerings. I could see this being a business opportunity that could be extremely lucrative for Andrew, especially with him getting in at the ground level. Standing between these two business leaders was Carrie. She was smiling into the camera, looking happy and proud, but readers were left to guess exactly who she was. Noticeably absent was any context for the woman whose name was featured in the photo's caption. Casual readers may not have noticed or thought that much about that missing information. That was not me—I was scouring this story for clues and answers.

It seemed to me that the story was mostly a PR piece with a sprinkle of news in it. Also missing from this piece was how Andrew met Miguel, and why he felt compelled to invest in both the personal and professional life of an unknown entrepreneur. Now, after the fact, I wasn't sure how much any of that even mattered. The bottom line was Andrew, Miguel, and Carrie were all connected to something that ultimately may have changed their lives. But what?

My progress, or lack of it, frustrated me. On the off chance that Galina actually showed up on Mongin Island, I wanted to be completely prepared and I wasn't. I didn't want her attitude, unease, her whole persona to prevent me from getting the answers I thought we needed and that she could and should provide. Although I had gone as far as I was physically and mentally able to, it did not feel like enough. Buddy had put himself to bed hours ago, and I finally had the good sense to follow him. Setting my alarm for the very next hour meant that I would be getting more of a nap than the deep sleep I needed. It didn't matter anyway, my mind was still churning on all that happened, all the conversations, all the things we learned, and all the strings that needed to be tied together.

In a blink, my room started to fill with gentle light, promising another beautiful Mongin Island day. My anticipation, excitement, curiosity, and maybe some anxiety helped pull me from my bed. After a quick cup of coffee, Buddy and I were in my cart and headed to the ferry landing. The crisp air pushed away the exhaustion and the frustration. I had to be ready, there would be no second chances to get this right.

As I pulled into the parking lot, Julie's black Suburban in the last row, away from the carts and luggage trolleys, was a welcome sight. "You must have had an early start!" I greeted her as she rolled down the driver's side window. Her presence felt a little like a lifeline. "The sheriff's boat is getting a workout this week!"

"I couldn't sleep. But also, I wanted to be here, just in case she shows up and you need me. Have to admit, I was pretty restless at home and not much use at the office either. Every twist and turn feels like we're burrowing deeper down that rabbit's hole I mentioned yesterday." The gentle breeze blew her long blonde curls and partially covered her face. I couldn't read her expression, but I could sense she felt as unsettled as I did. There were no clear paths in this investigation.

"I was going to say, it's like a house of doors. You walk through one, and another one suddenly appears in front of you." We both looked towards the water, trying to catch sight of the ferry, gauging how much time we had left together. "Julie, before she gets here, if she gets here, I have to tell you what I found. Last night, well, I made headway, but not as much as I had hoped for, to be honest."

Knowing our time alone could be limited, my priority was updating her on Galina and Andrew's foundation, the real estate investment, and the relationship with the entrepreneur Miguel Rosa.

I felt Julie's intensity as she consumed all this information. She was listening, watching, absorbing every word, every nuance. She knew me well enough by now, I had delivered enough of these updates that Julie intrinsically understood I was sharing only the highlights. I paused, mentally checking off each item. "So, after the day you had yesterday, this is not enough progress for you?" She smiled softly. "This Miguel Rosa, it's complicated."

"Tell me, before the boat arrives. What did you learn?"

"We got to the same place, just took a different route." Julie pulled out her small notebook and quickly flipped a dozen pages or so. Clicking her pen, she pointed to information in front of her that only she could see. "Rosa has a shady past, very shady. He arrived here from Mexico and while he is the entrepreneur you describe, we are exploring his other business dealings. And he keeps company with an undesirable cast of characters. More to come on that." She paused, again looking at the water. "Ferry's pulling in, let's see what happens if she's on this one. What are you doing with her?"

"She has not texted or called, so I don't know what to expect, really. I thought we would go to Books & Brew and talk. If she is willing, maybe we could walk the beach, see where Carrie died, and gauge her reaction. Kind of winging it here, a lot depends on her, to be honest. If she explodes like she did yesterday, we might not even make it out of the parking lot."

"Go ahead, I will follow behind you, I will be close by. And Carr, no matter what happens here, we are very close to the end, remember that." She returned her notebook to the front pocket of her shirt. "One last thing, you might be able to use this. Galina and Andrew met Miguel Rosa on a trip to an exclusive high-end Cancun resort. They were all guests there at the same time about six years ago. Mr. Rosa is not a struggling entrepreneur who needed a charitable donation, seed capital, or any other kind of financial assistance. Quite the opposite actually, so just keep that in mind."

I nodded. Walking to the top of the gangway, I stood alone. There weren't other islanders waiting for new arrivals. Likely the boat would be filled with our own residents returning from adventures on the mainland and beyond, or vendors coming to service island needs. It was generally too early for tourists and other visitors. The question would be answered quickly—would Galina be on this boat?

Chapter 23

She was not on the ferry.

I waited until all the crew stepped onto the dock, knowing that was the signal that all passengers had officially disembarked. They were busy preparing for the return trip to the mainland, and I was alone again. Standing and facing the water, almost willing her to appear, I was forced to face my own reality. I wanted answers for Carrie and all those who cared for her, of course. However, I wanted answers for us, the Mongin Island community. Carrie's death, and the disturbing circumstances around it, were not our Mongin. It likely was the reason I felt Tripp's struggle so personally. I felt it too and I wanted all of this gone.

Julie was out of her car, standing next to my cart and gently scratching Buddy's head. "He's so good, just waiting for you, curled up like a doughnut." It wasn't lost on me; I knew Julie was refocusing me and I smiled softly at her. "I'm bummed, I'm not going to fib." Buddy's tail thumped on the bench seat as I approached, happy we were together again.

"For sure, I get it. You thought we could wrap this up and move on with our lives. You know, it hardly ever works out that neatly. Not a lot of tying a bow on things in this line of work. Sorry to say, this isn't like what you see on TV."

She was right. I knew it, but I also needed that reminder. "It's ninety minutes until the next arrival. I'm going to walk this little guy on the beach unless you want to head to the store for a little while."

We agreed to meet back at the dock in about an hour and went our separate ways. She had other things that needed her attention and I wanted to clear my head and refocus properly. The time went quickly, but I felt lighter when I arrived at the ferry landing for the second time that morning. I could authentically say and mean that I was ready for the day. Julie was parked in the same spot, but this time I could see she was on her phone. I waved to her and walked quietly and confidently to the gangway, and was once again alone. I had already removed my navy quarter-zip pullover after my walk. Now seeing the water, my face felt the sun teasing one more perfect day as the ferry came into sight.

The ropes were thrown, and a handful of passengers disembarked. I held my breath, waiting to see if the crew would be next. Again, I saw her huge orange tote and colorful maxi dress before I saw her tiny frame. I turned to give Julie the signal, a sign that it was go time. She was too far away but I telepathically asked her to keep her eyes on me. Flooded with adrenaline, my heart pounded loudly in response to seeing who I thought would never come. She was also too far for me to see her face but while I waited for her approach, I worked hard to mask mine.

"Galina, welcome," I greeted her as she neared the top of the boat's ramp.

"Carr," she answered through a closed-lip smile. Gone was her exuberant greeting from yesterday. I don't think either of us knew what to expect from the other. Looking back on it now, it was clear we each had very different objectives. We did, however, have one thing in common. Each of us wanted to exert control and lead this meeting.

"Thank you for coming, we have a beautiful day for your first visit to Mongin. I thought we could head over—"

"I'm not staying long. Let's get to it, alright? You said you had things you wanted to know. Let's hear it," she interrupted.

"My cart is over there, let's head to a quiet place to chat." She was not going to unnerve me.

She silently followed me, taking two steps for every one of mine. There was an unsettled, chaotic energy vibrating from her. Her eyes landed on Buddy, and she immediately froze.

"Oh no, nope, no way. I can't, I'm not doing this. I hate dogs and they hate me. I am not riding with that!" She pointed furiously at Buddy, who had sat up and was happily wagging at the sound of our voices.

Given the Mongin culture, and how often Buddy accompanies me all around the island, it hadn't occurred to me that this would be the issue we faced. Out of all the things we needed to figure out and discuss, how to ride a few minutes down the road with the world's friendliest, most chill dog hadn't been on my list.

"Well, Galina, I can't leave him here. I promise you won't even know he is in the cart. He won't hurt you. He is a giant marshmallow."

"Everyone says that about their dogs and then they turn on you. You can't trust an animal, you absolutely cannot." She practically stomped her feet in place.

"You ride in the back, and he will stay up here with me. We have a very short ride. I promise you, he won't bother you." She climbed into the back seat, looking doubtful and hanging on to the side rails for dear life. Buddy sat back down, gently placing his head on my lap, completely without a care in the world.

We arrived at Books & Brew, and I asked her to wait outside while I got Buddy settled in my office. I took her silence as her agreement, thinking that ultimately, there weren't a lot of places she could go. What choice did she have? Now that Galina was on the island, she really couldn't leave easily.

Tripp was already setting up the store for the day. He greeted me as I threw open the store's front door. "Hey Carr, this is a surprise. I thought—"

"She's here, in the cart. But she hates dogs, I'm telling you, Tripp ..." I didn't finish that statement.

"Want me to bring Buddy home?" His voice trailed behind me as I led Buddy to his comfy dog bed and brought his water bowl into the room. Tripp appeared in the office doorway, watching me. "You're on a slow simmer, what's happened? This isn't about Galina's feelings about your dog. What's going on?"

"I'm not on steady footing, that's what's going on. I don't know what I'm doing. I feel like I know what happened, vaguely, and how it happened. I just don't know how to connect the strings, to tie it up. I'm just not sure how to prove it. There is just a lot, so many different things to consider, so many players in this. Julie says we are close, and I feel like she wants me to lead Galina into telling us her story. I feel like I know enough to poke at her, but I don't know, I wish I had more facts, more things I knew tied together."

"Trust your gut, remember? That's what you told me. Trust your gut, the words will come. How about you let her lead you? You don't have to be in control right now. You know what you need, let her take the wheel and drive. Once she gets started, you can help steer her."

The man was a genius. He understood people in the way I understood facts, figures, and processes. He saw this so clearly. "That is seriously the best idea I've heard this week. That's exactly what I should do. Let's see where she takes me, if she will take me."

"I'll make you both some peppermint tea and finish stocking the new arrivals. I will check in on this boy here but will stay in the background. You go and do this. I'll let Julie know what's happening here."

"Julie is on the island, she was at the dock. She told me she would stay close by."

"Just in case, I'll text her. You go on. I've got this." He waved his hand around, circling the room, and smiled reassuringly. His faith, and his words, propelled me forward. I knew at that moment I would take his suggestion.

Galina was right where I left her, except now she looked almost deflated. Slouched into the cart's rear-facing seat, her legs were crossed, and her arms were tucked in on both of her sides. She was wrapped tightly, protecting herself from something. The geometric pattern of her dress almost absorbed her. Seeing me, she straightened up, flipped her long, straight dark hair over her shoulders, and put on what I would later describe as her game face. Let her lead, I reminded myself.

"Galina, you're welcome to come inside. Buddy is in my office, behind a closed door. It will be just us and my colleague, Tripp. Come in and meet him."

We were soon settled in The Trading Floor with two mugs of tea. Tripp had come and gone, disappearing into the front room. In the stillness of the shop, I knew he could hear every word and I was happy knowing we were in it together.

"Thanks for coming over, Galina. It was hard to really talk yesterday, with how busy it was and all. I am glad for this chance now." We were sitting on either side of the farm table. She looked at me blankly. It became clear she wanted me to say something, maybe anything, so she would have a reason to react. I continued, "I know we both have some questions, so please ask me anything, what can I tell you?"

"Tell me? What are you talking about? You came to find me, not the other way around. You invited me here to find out more about Carrie. So, Carr, what do you want to know?" She sat back in her chair and crossed her arms in front of her.

So, this was how it was going to go. So much for letting her lead. I would take Tripp's advice and trust my gut—it was now telling me to run a different play. "When you told me you couldn't give me what I wanted, what did you mean? What do you think I want?"

She jumped at the chance to set me straight. "You want me to fill you in on Carrie, right? Tell you all about this girl, what she was like, what our relationship was, right? You want me to tell you about why I had to talk to her. Well, it's a long story. Let's just say that we have a mutual friend who had a message for Carrie. Since I was in the area, and we heard Carrie would be here, too, well, it just made sense that I would pass along the message."

"Was this friend your husband, Andrew, or one of his business partners, like Miguel? Which friend are you referring to?" She blinked quickly and shifted in her seat. She said nothing, so I continued, "Seems like an awful lot of energy to casually deliver a message. You had to talk to her mom, work out the details of the meeting. Wouldn't it have been easier just to call her, or text her, with your message? Seems like a lot of effort on someone else's behalf for a former co-worker you haven't spoken to in years. What was the message? Must have been pretty important that you delivered it in person to someone whom you didn't even consider your friend."

Honestly, it seemed that a series of questions was the last thing she expected because her hands shook as she wrapped them around the mug in front of her. Her dark brown eyes were fixed on the tea Tripp had made and after a long minute of silence, she answered.

"Miguel has nothing to do with this. It was Andrew's message. They worked together and—"

"Do you deliver messages to all of Andrew's mistresses or just Carrie?"

She was beginning to understand that today was a completely different day than yesterday. I now knew a lot more about her, about them, and felt I had a pretty good understanding of what may have happened.

"Andrew's transgression is none of your business. If this is what you wanted to ask me, I didn't need to come to this dump." She looked around the room, and it was clear she was not impressed.

Maybe she mistakenly thought her opinion about my store, the island, or anything at all mattered to me.

"Galina, I think you know I didn't ask you here to drill you about the state of your marriage. However, it is relevant because Andrew and Carrie worked together on projects outside of the work they did for the company. I read the articles, I saw the pictures. I know Carrie was more than just an employee. Let's start there."

"Carrie was looking to advance her career. She would have done anything that Andrew asked. She did do anything, everything he asked. She is not entirely to blame, as I know better than anyone, he is very persuasive. And he's used to getting his own way. There is something about him. His power, I guess, he never doubts it. He commands the room, which is what everyone always says about him."

She went on, "Things obviously got messy in the office. Everyone knew, including local management and the people at the highest levels of our company. Andrew's situation put the company at risk for litigation. We all knew it, although I don't think that was what Carrie was thinking. The risk was there, nonetheless. So, he was moved on, quietly of course. And with full benefits, including glowing recommendations."

"Moved on? He was terminated?" I interrupted. 'Moved on' seemed too gentle of a description considering all the damage that had been done.

She shook her head, "No, not officially, of course. He resigned and found other opportunities. My role, my career, there was also over. There would be no way I could stay and face everyone. I worked in HR, I mean, right?" She looked at me. "It was hard to enforce corporate policies that my own husband didn't abide by. All of it was very humiliating, public, and messy."

"Andrew begged forgiveness and you know, we always had an understanding. We are a team, for better or worse. I can't resist him, no matter how I try. We separated, but in retrospect that was likely more about appearances. I was embarrassed, angry, God, so angry at all of it. And this separation was his public punishment. My friends, well, they all loved that he finally got what was owed to him. None of them were huge Andrew fans. Turns out, it didn't last long. He had a new role in just a few months, and eventually that position was relocated to their Florida office. He asked me to move with him, officially start again, reimagine and reinvent our team. And well, that was that."

Tripp appeared in the doorway. "Sorry to interrupt. Helen is here, and she needs to speak to you urgently."

"Tripp, is this—"

"Carr, Galina, pardon this interruption. This will only take a minute, but you're needed. Now."

Something was wrong, Tripp never spoke like this. "Excuse me, Galina, I will be right back." She nodded and sat back in her chair.

This break came at the most inopportune time, it gave her time I didn't want her to have. She was just getting into her story.

"What's going on?" I whispered to Tripp. "I am just getting her into a little corner, we were just starting to make progress!"

"It's this." He turned his computer toward me. "Helen's on the front porch. You know how she worries about things from the mainland spilling onto the island with the tourists, and so on. After Barb told her that we had a few more Atlanta arrivals this week, she commented that there have been quite a few people from there over the last few months, and she hoped that they would not be bringing all the city issues here."

"Tripp, that's ridiculous. I'm sorry, I don't mean to be disrespectful to Helen, but come on, Atlanta is like any other major city. It just happens to be the one closest to us. What big-city issues are vacationers going to bring to us? Carrie's death had nothing to do with where she lived. People from Atlanta and everywhere else have been visiting here for decades. This is nothing new."

"I know, I know. She worries, right? She worries about everything, but she told me about an Atlanta-based major drug ring that was just broken up a few weeks ago. It was an East Coast hub for part of the opioid drug-running operations. Cracking it took the DEA and all the agencies. You know how she loves all this stuff, right? Helen loves true crime shows, watches them all. She reads the police procedural novels. She was saying our island was a perfect place for a criminal to hide and that Barb had said the same thing when y'all were looking for Carrie."

Regrettably, I was impatient and saw bigger gains in the room I had just left. "Let's finish here today and then we can help Helen." I turned to head back to The Trading Floor.

"It's Helen who has helped you." His words stopped me. "Look at this, start about a quarter of the way down the page."

His finger pointed to the exact spot on his screen. I didn't get beyond the third sentence when my mouth dropped, and my eyes popped. "This is the story she was talking about," Tripp said quietly.

For the second time that day, I threw open the wood and glass front door of Books & Brew. Helen was sitting on one of the rockers on the porch, a glass of lemonade in her hand. Her eyes fixed on Old Port Passage Way, keeping track of the comings and goings. "Helen, let me hug you. I owe you both an apology and a huge thank you. I will explain it all. But come here, thank you!" I bent down to scoop her up.

"I'm not going to refuse you, but I'm not sure what the fuss is." She stood and didn't finish her thought. I embraced her sincerely, ashamed of my dismissiveness. I couldn't recall being this physically close to her and for the first time, I noticed how small she really was. Her words and her presence made her almost larger than life but in this brief hug, I could feel her bony shoulders and how slight she was.

"I know you have a guest, but I do have a few things I want to ask you. I'll stop by later, again. I'm not sure that the books for my club will work and ..."

And just like that, we were back to normal. Helen was never at a loss with her concerns, questions, and opinions.

"Definitely, come by later or tonight. I will get your questions answered and your books straightened out. Thank you, Helen." I turned and almost ran back to The Trading Floor.

"Tripp, please, text Julie," I threw at him as I quickly passed.

"Already done, boss." As I looked back, I saw him smile at me and then mouthed "Go get her!" right before I turned back to Galina.

"Sorry, Galina." She startled as I reentered the room. "That took a few minutes longer than I expected."

"Is everything okay? That man seemed pretty concerned."

I smiled, "All is well, yes. Sorry about all that. Tripp just needed to bring something to my attention."

"Your face is flushed, you don't look well. What's wrong with you?" she poked at me. "Are you ill?"

Returning to my ladder-back chair, I spoke directly with both my words and the look that passed between us. She was not going to create any distraction for me. "Nothing is wrong, just a little bit of running around. Where were we? I think we were talking about your

move to Florida, and your separation from Andrew. Please, continue."
It was the excitement of knowing one piece to this, having one more
thing click into place that was making my cheeks burn. She would
find that out soon enough.

"I think you get the gist of it, right? We obviously reconciled. The
move to Florida allowed me freedoms I didn't have in my corporate
career. We came to an understanding, as the saying goes."

I bet, I thought to myself. I could only imagine that understanding.

"The Lowcountry has some of the most picturesque coastal beauty
on the Atlantic, in my opinion. It never gets old to me, the sunsets,
the beaches, the dirt roads, and our palm trees, all of it. What brings
you and Andrew back here so regularly? You made quite a name for
yourself at the coffee shop, the barista recognized your picture right
away. She said you visit the area pretty frequently. Why?"

"It's not that often, it's the same as what we always did. We always
traveled to this area, it's nothing new. I think, well, no disrespect here,
but I think you're overthinking these things, making something out
of ordinary life."

Ignoring that, I went on with the pleasantries, although I was
instantly grateful I had enough previous professional experience and
Julie's guidance to recognize the deflection for what it was. Galina
was uncomfortable, likely because I was getting close to some sore
spot.

"Well, it seems pretty new that you're spending so much time in
that one spot of the mainland, enough time that you're making several visits to the same coffee shop each day."

"Well, the coffee shop is also new, so I couldn't have been there
previously. Anyway, it's for my clients. Clients like meeting in that
store. I have quite a—"

I held up my hand, already reaching my limit of her pushback. She
had an answer for everything but very little of it was helpful. "Galina,
please, you're trying to tell me that marketing resume design service
in a tourist hot spot is the focal point of your business? This can't
possibly be the reason you're traveling to this area. It's not to hang out

regularly at a coffee shop. We both know this is just not your main demographic for your services. What's the real reason?"

Her dark brown eyes were a window into her thoughts. She blinked furiously again, and for a long minute, I thought she was a flight risk. I almost would have bet she was going to walk right out the front door just to get away from me. But looking back on it, I think she was deciding how she was going to navigate our time together, trying to determine how much I knew and how much she could hide. The only reason she came to Mongin was to find out what we knew. I thought this was true then and I still believe it to this day.

"Your work is not bringing you here. It's something to do while you're here. But Andrew's travel is purposeful, and I think it's to meet with Jett Jepson. Is Andrew running for office?"

Chapter 24

Galina gasped. "Why would you ask that?"

"Tripp found the picture of y'all at the fancy fundraiser on the mainland and that got me thinking about Jett Jepson. I would never have been able to recall his name but as soon as Tripp said it, I recognized it. I know Jett is a rainmaker, so to speak, having raised money for lots of candidates. And I guess he helps campaigns strategize. Jett's face, it's pretty memorable, right? When I saw a few pictures, I remembered seeing him with lots of other people running at the state level and a few in national races. That's why I asked. Why else would they be together? And it makes sense that's why you would be frequently visiting the Lowcountry—Jett lives here."

"Andrew—he has big dreams like always, but no, I wouldn't say he is running for office."

"But he is considering it, would you say that?"

She shrugged her shoulders and her eyebrows arched as she looked away. I knew we would soon be interrupted by customers, so it was time to put the pieces all together. In our silence, I wondered if we were both thinking the same thing. Were we both running through all the different parts of Carrie's story, trying to figure out how close we were to the end, to knowing the truth? That idea energized me, propelled me, but Galina looked like she was fading in front of me.

"I know you must be anxious to get back to the mainland. How about a walk on the beach before you go? It wouldn't be a visit to Mongin if you didn't get to feel the sand under your feet. What do you say?"

"I'm not here for a day of fun and sun, I came to answer your questions, which I did. And it was lovely to officially meet you."

It took some convincing. I was as charming as I knew how to be, which may not be saying all too much. In reality, I think she knew I was her ride to the ferry. Unless she wanted to walk a few miles, all her debating was just posturing. She ultimately relented. I didn't give her time to change her mind. As we walked through the store, I ever so casually told Tripp where we were headed. He knew what to do and picked up his phone, texting Julie while concurrently appearing completely disinterested in this sudden change of events. Tripp texted me our new mantra, "Trust your gut."

"Kick off your sandals, you can leave them here, in the cart. No one will touch anything," I encouraged Galina a few minutes later when we had parked. The ride to the beach was short, but still long enough for me to know exactly where we would head together. The tide was still out, the powdery beach was wide, and we could walk without ever touching the water. She slipped on a pair of oversized tortoise sunglasses. It was impossible to see her eyes, but I noticed that both of her hands were curled into tight fists, silently telling me she was ready for a fight.

"Let's go this way," I directed her away from the Rosemont Inn and toward the turtle nesting area. She followed my lead, unknowingly getting closer to what she would never want to see. "Isn't this beautiful, it's perfect right?" I was calmly, casually, inviting her to let her guard down.

Dismissively, she almost agreed, "Mmm, yeah, it's much like areas on the mainland." The hair tie that had served as one of her bracelets now trapped her hair in a high ponytail. She looked younger and more vulnerable. Looking back on it, I think we both knew something big was coming. Preparing to dive off my own information cliff without being able to see or touch the bottom, I took one steady, long look at the ocean and knew it was time.

"Galina, thank you for the time we had together today. I know you didn't have to come to Mongin, you didn't have to answer my questions. Remember Barb told you that we are working on a project of a different kind? I need your help to finish our work. This won't take long, but—"

"What help can I provide? I don't know your project, your work. I barely know you. Take me back to the boat, I answered everything you asked. I don't know—"

I stopped her from lecturing me. "Not everything, I haven't asked everything, yet." Gradually the day had been turning cloudier, but as we walked down the beach the sun was still making an effort, hidden as it was behind gray clouds. I looked toward the horizon and I saw a couple, standing alone, near the water's edge, with their backs to us. They would be my mile-marker. I knew Galina and I would say all we had to before we got beyond them.

"Here's what I think, Galina, and you can certainly disagree. For someone I never met before yesterday, I've spent a lot of time and energy trying to understand you, and what I think you did." She stopped walking and turned toward me but said nothing. Her back was facing the water and as I turned toward her, I spotted blonde curls flying in the wind. Julie. We would make our way closer to her, so she could take over when the time was right.

I continued, "Your husband is a narcissist and you've lived in his shadow for decades. You're a fixer, right? He bulldozes things down, and you run behind him, cleaning up. In this case, I think Andrew got involved with Miguel after you all met in Cancun, right?"

She seemed surprised that I knew this much, "Yes, we met on that trip. They both have an entrepreneurial spirit. They clicked immediately."

"But the poor, struggling start-up was kind of a facade, right? Miguel Rosa has quite a few successful business ventures, including the imported food products. Mr. Rosa, as it turns out, is quite the entrepreneur, but unfortunately, his biggest venture seems to be an illegal one. His arrest must have been very disturbing for you and Andrew, considering the plans for the future and all. It made the Atlanta newspapers and the national media, too, after all. I mean, if our friend Helen could find it, any of Andrew's opponents could find it, too. The work with Jett Jepson would have been in jeopardy, right? Consorting with the leader of a massive drug ring is probably not a campaign talking point."

Galina started walking slowly but stopped a few feet later, "We had no idea about that side of Miguel. Andrew just wanted to invest in his business and help with the cost of housing his staff—which were all Miguel's relatives and family friends. That's it, that's all it was."

"That's not true and you know it. The real estate investment, it wasn't for Miguel's struggling family. It was for drug trafficking—right there in the middle of just a regular old neighborhood. It was hiding in plain sight. Sure, maybe Miguel's family benefited from those homes, that's for the police to figure out, but the intended purpose is clear. Andrew knew, and maybe you both did. And Carrie must have known or at least you thought she did. That's what all this is about. It started with the payments to Carrie, month after month, year after year. Hush money. You bought her silence. That's where it started, but that is certainly not where it ended."

We were only a few feet from Deputy Julie and Lieutenant Cole, close enough for them to hear what I hoped Galina would say. "Galina, I think you knew very well that Andrew was paying Carrie to stay silent about everything she learned about Miguel Rosa. For years, that was your arrangement, but with his recent arrest, the news stories, and the unwanted publicity, Carrie was a risk you weren't willing to tolerate. You needed to get rid of people who knew the full story, who were there from the beginning. Did Andrew tell you to eliminate her, or was this your decision?"

"I want to show you something up here, near the dune grass. Come this way." I pointed to the spot where we had found Carrie.

Galina kept any questions she may have had to herself. She followed me, obediently, silently, and heavily. The fight in her was gone and I believed she surrendered to the reality of what was coming. I noticed Julie and Cole were following behind us, at a distance. Clearing the small hill, we came to the patch of crushed grass near the wooden stakes protecting the turtle's nest. No one expected to encounter Tracy sitting in the spot where Carrie had been found. Navigating this was not something I was ready for, and I immediately hoped it would not put Tracy or our ability to hear Galina's story at risk.

"I wanted to see the spot, I wanted to say goodbye. We walked this beach together and it feels wrong to be leaving without her. I don't know that we will ever understand this. I just—" Tracy finally truly saw us and realized it was not Barb with me. She immediately stopped speaking and stood.

"Tracy, Galina is going to tell us now, what happened, how it happened. Right?"

"Galina? No, oh no, what did you do?" Tracy screamed. Her rage exploded.

We waited, but Galina was frozen to the spot where she stood, and no words came from her. I began for her, "Tracy, we learned that Andrew was fired from his role at the company where they all worked, Carrie, Galina, and Andrew. He was asked to leave over his inappropriate behavior with Carrie. Andrew and Galina moved to Florida, to begin their life again. As it turns out, Andrew decided he wanted a career in politics, so he has been working with a campaign strategist and fundraiser on the mainland."

Tracy's eyes moved quickly between me and Galina. She was watching, listening with such intensity, not just for herself, but so that she could share it all with Mary Frances and Annabelle. Even in these most difficult circumstances, she was thinking of her friends. I continued, "Andrew, and tangentially Carrie, got involved in an investment deal with someone who would ultimately be arrested as a drug ring leader."

"Carrie was involved in a drug ring? A drug lord? What are you saying? That just is not possible. I will not stand here and listen to this garbage." Tracy shook her head, as if she could stop the words from attaching to her.

"Carrie didn't know, she didn't know about Miguel. She just thought she was helping to find his relatives and friends a home. She didn't know, she was just wrapped up in Andrew," Galina finally spoke. "Carrie did what Andrew wanted, what he asked of her. She did it and he paid her for help, the work that was done outside of the company. Eventually, I think she sensed something didn't add up in Andrew's story. She was smart, we all know that. Unfortunately, that was her downfall. She was smart and she knew right from wrong. She begged for my forgiveness, and I gave it to her. I believed her, she knew her relationship with Andrew was wrong. She showed more humility and regret than Andrew ever did. But still, she knew about Miguel and Andrew, she knew too much."

I let that sink in for a minute. "So, you placed your coffee order on your phone app once you and Carrie met by The Captain's Deck. Your name was on Carrie's cup because you ordered the drinks. We found Carrie's cup on the resort property, that's how I knew. It was you. You ordered her drink and then you slipped in the rosary pea, or more specifically its seed, the abrin. It's your ring, right? I noticed the small hinge on the top, near that bezel. I read about rings like this, but never saw a poison ring in real life. That's what it is, right?"

"This is a family heirloom," Galina said, twisting the ring around and around on her finger. "My grandmother wore it, and legend has it she kept snuff in it. I knew it would work because it was just the right size for the amount of abrin I needed. All I had to do was open the top and tap it into her drink. She was so uncomfortable, and the store was so crowded, distractions were everywhere. It was done before we walked to the counter where she grabbed her straw. Honestly, I could hardly believe how easy it was. One tap and that was it. It was surreal, the store was so crowded, but no one knew my secret."

She went on. Now that she started telling her story, it seemed she couldn't stop. "Carrie's mom was only too happy to help arrange our meeting. I told her I needed to verify some information for a company payout that had not been properly processed. It was an added plus that she was going to be here on the island. I didn't know that at first, but it seemed like it was fate. The poor woman had no idea who I was or that I didn't work for the company anymore. She told me that Carrie was going to the Lowcountry for vacation, and I shared that I was, too. Fate, right?"

"Once she called me back with the date and time, I knew what I was going to do. Everything was set. Rosary pea grows wildly in the open land on the side of the road, not far from where we live. When I asked the locals about the violet-colored flowers and their pods that look like lady bugs, they told me all about it and how we can't plant it anymore because it's too invasive. Wherever it grows, it takes over. Made it all so easy to find what I needed. No one batted an eye with me cutting off a few pods, no one even noticed."

"Galina, you thought you could just set these wheels in motion, and Carrie would die here. Did you think we would not solve this? How did you think this would end?" I wanted to know.

She disregarded my questions and focused only on her story, what she wanted us to know. "I am sure Carrie was curious, and it probably was the only reason she agreed to meet me, she probably thought there was some news about Andrew. Her mother knew nothing about any of that, but Carrie could read between the lines. It was all so easy, everything went as planned. I knew when you told me that Carrie had been ill, it was likely all over, but you didn't tell me she was dead. That's what I came for today, I wanted to know if Carrie would finally be out of our way."

"So, you thought she would just die here. Did you think we wouldn't want to know what happened to her? After all we went through with you and your husband, did you really think you would poison her, and we wouldn't all want to know what happened?" Tracy demanded. "You should know better than anyone how much we invested in trying to get her away from you and Andrew."

"Yes, absolutely, I knew you would want to know, but did I think you would be able to figure it out? No, of course not. You didn't figure any of it out. You just thought she shouldn't have been with a married man. You didn't know half of what went on, she didn't tell you everything." She spoke so dismissively to Tracy that I wondered if Galina actually cared about anything but protecting Andrew. "Like I said, I didn't know she would be here, but when I found out she was going to be on vacation on this island, it seemed like the right time, and it certainly was easier for me. I thought she would be sick, here on the island. With no hospital, there would be no antidote. I thought she would pass during the night of what would look like an exotic virus or some weird illness. And that would be that."

Galina looked from Tracy to me, to Julie and Cole, and spoke to no one in particular, "This, well, all of it, is a special kind of heartache. It's the loss of what could be, what should be. It wasn't Carrie's fault, but she paid for trusting the wrong person and then not being able to live with it. That's what made her a problem for us, she wanted to fix her mistakes. Funny, that was her own biggest mistake. Her decision made us all lose, and now all of us have a special heartache to bear."

Tracy lunged at Galina, but Cole caught her before she made contact. To this day, I can't unhear the scream that came from her as she understood all of Galina's words.

"Galina, I am Deputy Julie, and you're under arrest for the murder of Carrie Nichols."

Chapter 25

After Deputy Julie and Lieutenant Cole took Galina away on Saturday, I stayed with Tracy for a long time. We sat on the beach until she was ready to head back to the cottage and narrate Carrie's story. We covered a lot of ground together as Tracy finally was able to open up. She no longer needed to protect Carrie, like she had been doing for years, trying to guard against the harm to Carrie's reputation and the effect it had on Carrie herself. I learned a lot about Carrie, but I learned much more about friendship and community.

This group was made up of true friends. They didn't give up on each other when times were tough, they showed up for each other. They were each other's advocates, but they also held each other accountable. Each woman had her own talents, which were respected and admired by the group. But at the same time, they kept each other's confidences. I left them as they processed all that Tracy shared, knowing I was not needed. Tracy would answer their questions and comfort them in a way I would never be able to.

It helped to stabilize the community to hear, even at this collective low point, all the ways our neighbors stepped forward for this group of friends. The many volunteers, the donated food, the offers of help, and the thoughts and prayers, all were a part of a culture on which we could count. Fortunately, it was not reserved only for island residents. If you were on Mongin, you were part of Mongin and the island community stood with you. This is what makes this home to people, sometimes as soon as their first visit here. People who didn't know Mongin would say it was our "southern hospitality," and to a certain extent it was. But it went beyond that. Deciding to live on a bridgeless island without all the parts of daily life you may take for granted on the mainland made you understand quickly your life would be a balance of being independent and resourceful while also being able to ask for and receive help.

A few days later, most of us had digested the information about Carrie, Galina, Andrew, and even Miguel. It no longer stung to speak about it all. But that didn't mean the island had healed. Many of us learned about rosary pea for the very first time and now knew it was somehow very easy to get your hands on this lethal poison, since it grew prolifically in the region. We learned about a tangential Mongin connection to a national drug ring. We also learned that sometimes it is the smallest detail, like the name on a coffee order, that can be a clue used to help solve a murder mystery. These were not the usual parts of island life. Many of us had heard the news and understood the series of events, but all of it still left us unsettled. People were trying to move forward in their own ways. Some of us spent time going over the details with neighbors, adding color or tales of participation or contribution. Others connected with friends and family, recognizing their good fortune of having their loved ones with them.

Hetty, the General Store's owner and manager, was the one person who many of us saw frequently. Her's was the only store on the island, and it is not unusual for islanders to stop in for one or two groceries, a package of batteries, or a miscellaneous, oddball thing that they need. The general store had a small quantity of a wide variety of items and was often the next stop if a neighbor wasn't able to loan you that one thing you were looking for.

But Tuesday was usually the day most islanders tried to make a trip to the General Store, regardless of whether they really needed anything. Miss Lucy delivered her famous pies on Tuesdays, and they were not to be missed. We never knew what she would bring and after all these months, I learned it didn't really matter. They were all delicious works of art. She baked what she felt, what she thought people needed. The goodness wasn't just the combination of her ingredients. She lovingly presented them with rope crusts or crumb-covered tops, all baked to be golden brown. You could smell the sweet scents of her arrival before you stepped foot onto the store's white wooden front steps or pulled open the screen door. The ceiling fans didn't do much to shoo out the humidity, but they did help spread the cinnamon sugar air.

This Tuesday was a little different. Instead of just taking a chance, arriving when you could, and seeing islanders coming and going as their schedule allowed, many of us received a text message from Hetty, asking us to stop by around 9:30 a.m. I pulled into the small lot right after Barb.

"I thought you were having your meeting with the handyman today for that rental's deck you wanted to repair?" I greeted her as we each climbed out of our carts. "I could have picked you up!"

"That's tomorrow," she answered. "I didn't realize that there was a whole thing going on, I thought Hetty just needed a favor." Barb's hand was on her forehead, shielding her eyes from the sun as she looked around at our neighbors. "Have any idea about this?"

"Nope, none at all. Honestly, I thought the same thing. I wonder—"

Before I finished my thought, we heard the rattle of Miss Lucy's cart. Hitched behind it was her silver catering trailer. "Now this is very interesting, very interesting indeed." Barb looked at me, smiling brightly and pointing to Miss Lucy.

A few more carts pulled in, people were parked here and there. Moving carefully around each other, we gathered in small groups, comparing our messages from Hetty and our theories as to why we were called to the store. Others went to help Miss Lucy unpack her inventory.

The screen door squeaked open and Hetty stood on the store's landing like she was the grand marshal of a small-town parade. "Morning everyone! Good to see you!" She shouted over the sounds of tires crunching pine cones and the beeping of carts backing up. People on the left side of the store were trying to make space for someone else to squeeze in across from the picnic area. "Everyone, can we have your attention? Miss Lucy has asked you all here this morning. Miss Lucy, come on up, please."

Miss Lucy passed a few more pies to Helen and wiped her hands on the blue half-apron tied at her waist. Without saying it, we all knew something was coming. The air was filled with anticipation, and truth be told, I think some people were slightly anxious about an announcement made in a public forum like this. What else could be happening that we all needed to be here at the same time?

With her left hand on the railing, Miss Lucy climbed the few wooden stairs purposefully. She turned around slowly. The sterling silver shell necklace she always wore shined in the sun. A sudden still-ness circled us, and Miss Lucy had our complete attention. When she spoke, we listened.

"Look at you, you beautiful people, my people," she started gently. I immediately felt the warmth from her voice and saw how her dark eyes sparkled as she took in the sight of us before her. "We have been through it, this week, we have been through it all. Isn't that right?"

Her crowd murmured their agreement, and she went on, "As you know, my family, we have been on this island for generations. Some of my kin never left this island, not one time. We have seen it all, wars, crops that failed, hurricanes, troubled times, good times, my family has seen it all."

She looked us over, seemingly searching for someone or some-thing in the crowd. Without acknowledging anyone, she continued, "My pies and goodies, those recipes are from my mother, grandmas, and aunties. They taught me to bake and showed me how to make people feel loved and cared for through the food I prepared for them. When you come here, every week, to buy my pies, you are showing me how you care for me, too. This is why I do this every week."

A few ladies standing under a small tree's shade clapped and cheered. "We *do* love you, Lucy!"

Miss Lucy smiled, "Well, I know we are hurting, I know it has been hard to hear some of these stories these past days and I know it's been upsetting, especially for those of us who helped figure out what happened. But we are here now, and we are going to have some pies today. More and more pies. I baked and baked for you because we needed to celebrate us, we needed to be here together, with us. Do you want to know why?"

With her arms spread wide she said, "I called you, I asked you to come and you came. All of you, you came. You just showed up, without knowing why, without asking what we needed or wanted. Me and Hetty, well, we asked for you and here you are. And that's what we do, we show up. We are for each other. We are here now because each of us cares for each of us. The bad things that happen, the evil people bring here doesn't change who we are. And, we are going to remember that and celebrate that goodness, that kindness. That is what makes this place, this wonderful, special place, our home."

She smiled and threw her hands in the air. "Who is ready for pie?"

The crowd roared and cheered. We were definitely ready for pie. We were ready to celebrate that we have this island community filled with all the different people who make this place home. The area in front of the store was soon buzzing with activity. The curiosity and hesitation that had been in the air when we first arrived had been replaced with joy and fun. We would enjoy the treat of Miss Lucy's baking and of simply being together.

"I don't know how she does it, this woman, she's incredible." Barb looked at me, grinning. "Miss Lucy is talented *and* wise."

I looked around at the crowd, busy setting up tables and chairs, making room for each other, slicing pies, and passing plates. "You're right about that. She is talented and wise, and we are lucky, so very lucky to call Mongin Island home."

Don't miss book 1 of
The Island Mysteries series!

Join Carr and her friends at the very beginning of their adventures on Mongin Island in *All Is Now Lost*. When Carr and Barb go to Governor's Point to take the perfect photo for the walls of Books & Brew, what they discover in the waterfront neighborhood sets off a mystery that catapults Carr into Mongin's once-turbulent history.

THE ISLAND MYSTERIES

It is my sincerest hope that you enjoyed *A Special Kind of Heartache*, reconnecting with old friends like Carr, Barb, and Tripp and imagining time on Mongin Island.

As part of The Island Mysteries series, Carr and her friends will have more adventures on their beloved island. Stay tuned for Book 3 and please check my website for updates and the opportunity to subscribe to my insider's newsletter. All of the latest news can be found at TheIslandMysteries.com.

Thank you for sharing this journey with me!

Wishing you lots of island magic,

Laura Elizabeth